Gabrielle Zevin was raise[d] [...] [...] to the
library like it was church. She suspects that is why she
became a writer. Her career began at age fourteen when an
angry letter to her local newspaper about a Guns N' Roses
concert resulted in a job as a music critic. Over eight novels
for adults and young people, she has written about female
soldiers in Iraq, mafia princesses in retro-future New York
City, teenage girls in the afterlife, talking dogs, amnesiacs and
the difficulties of loving one person over many years. She is
probably best known for her first novel, *Elsewhere*, which has
been translated into twenty-five languages. She is also the
screenwriter of the cult hit *Conversations with Other Women*.

'Delightful! I read [it] in one sitting. This novel has humor,
romance, a touch of suspense, but most of all love – love of
books and bookish people and, really, all of humanity in its
imperfect glory' Eowyn Ivey, author of *The Snow Child*

'I read this book in one big greedy gulp. A charming and
funny love letter to the written word - it will leave you smiling
and with a large lump in your throat' Natasha Solomons, best-
selling author of *Mr Rosenblum's List* and *The Novel in the Viola*

'*The Storied Life of A. J. Fikry* reminds us what saves us all from
a life of loneliness and isolation: our sense of empathy; our
ability to love and be loved; our willingness to care and be
cared for. Gabrielle Zevin has written a wonderful, moving,
endearing story of redemption and transformation that will
sing in your heart for a very, very long time' Garth Stein,
author of *The Art of Racing in the Rain*

THE
STORIED LIFE
OF A. J. FIKRY

Gabrielle Zevin

ABACUS

First published in the United States in 2014 by Algonquin
First published in Great Britain in 2014 by Little, Brown
as *The Collected Works of A. J. Fikry*
This paperback edition published in 2015 by Abacus

A CIP catalogue record for this book
is available from the British Library.

ISBN 978-0-349-14107-7
Export ISBN 978-0-349-14113-8

Typeset in Baskerville by M Rules
Printed and bound in Great Britain by
Clays Ltd, St Ives plc

Papers used by Abacus are from well-managed forests
and other responsible sources.

MIX
Paper from
responsible sources
FSC
www.fsc.org   FSC® C104740

Abacus
An imprint of
Little, Brown Book Group
100 Victoria Embankment
London EC4Y 0DY

An Hachette UK Company
www.hachette.co.uk

www.littlebrown.co.uk

For my parents, who furnished my formative
years with books, and for the boy, who bought me
The Stories of Vladimir Nabokov all those winters ago.

come on, sweetheart
let's adore one another
before there is no more
of you and me.
                       – Rumi

Contents

THE
STORIED LIFE
OF A. J. FIKRY

PART I

Lamb to the Slaughter

1953/Roald Dahl

Wife kills husband with frozen leg of lamb, then disposes of the 'weapon' by feeding it to the cops. Serviceable-enough Dahl offering, though Lambiase questioned whether a professional housewife could successfully cook a leg of lamb in the manner described – i.e., without thawing, seasoning or marinade. Wouldn't this result in tough, unevenly cooked meat? My business isn't cooking (or crime), but if you dispute this detail, the whole story begins to unravel. Despite this reservation, it makes the cut because of a girl I know who loved James and the Giant Peach *once upon a time.*

– A. J. F.

On the ferry from Hyannis to Alice Island, Amelia Loman paints her nails yellow and, while waiting for them to dry, skims her predecessor's notes. 'Island Books, approximately $350,000 per annum in sales, the better portion of that in the summer months to folks on holiday,' Harvey Rhodes reports. 'Six hundred square feet of selling space. No full-time employees other than owner. Very small children's section. Fledgling online presence. Poor community outreach. Inventory emphasizes the literary, which is good for us, but Fikry's tastes are very specific, and without Nic, he can't be counted on to hand-sell. Luckily for him, Island's the only game in town.' Amelia yawns – she's nursing a slight hangover – and wonders if one persnickety little bookstore will be worth such a long trip. By the time her nails have hardened, her relentlessly bright-sided nature has kicked in: *Of course it's worth it!* Her specialty is persnickety little bookstores and the particular breed that runs them. Her talents also include multi-tasking, selecting the right wine at dinner (and the coordinating skill, tending friends who've had too much to drink), houseplants, strays and other lost causes.

As she steps off the ferry, her phone rings. She doesn't recognize the number – none of her friends use their phones as phones any more. Still, she is glad for the diversion and she doesn't want to become the kind of person who thinks that good news can only come from calls one was already expecting and callers one already knows. The caller turns out to be Boyd Flanagan, her third online dating failure, who had taken her to the circus about six months back.

'I tried sending you a message a few weeks ago,' he says. 'Did you get it?'

She tells him that she recently switched jobs so her devices have been screwed up. 'Also, I've been rethinking the whole idea of online dating. Like whether it's really for me.'

Boyd doesn't seem to hear that last part. 'Would you want to go out again?' he asks.

Re: their date. For a time, the novelty of the circus had distracted from the fact that they had nothing in common. By the end of dinner, the greater truth of their incompatibility had been revealed. Perhaps it should have been obvious from their inability to reach consensus on an appetizer or from his main-course admission that he disliked 'old things' – antiques, houses, dogs, people. Still, Amelia had not allowed herself to be certain until dessert, when she'd asked him about the book that had had the greatest influence on his life, and he'd replied *Principles of Accounting, Part II*.

Gently, she tells him no, she would rather not go out again.

She can hear Boyd breathing, fluttery and irregular. She worries that he might be crying. 'Are you all right?' she asks.

'Don't patronize me.'

Amelia knows she should hang up, but she doesn't. Some part of her wants the story. What is the point of bad dates if not to have amusing anecdotes for your friends? 'Excuse me?'

'You'll notice I didn't call you right away, Amelia,' he says. 'I didn't call you because I had met someone better, and when that didn't work out, I decided to give you a second chance. So don't be thinking you're superior. You've got a decent smile, I'll give you that, but your teeth are too big and so is your ass and you're not twenty-five any more even if you drink like you are. You shouldn't look a gift horse in the mouth.' The gift horse begins to cry. 'I'm sorry. I'm really sorry.'

'It's fine, Boyd.'

'What's wrong with me? The circus was fun, right? And I'm not so bad.'

'You were great. The circus was very creative.'

'But there must be a reason you don't like me. Be honest.'

At this point, there are many reasons not to like him. She picks one. 'Do you remember when I said I worked in publishing and you said you weren't much of a reader?'

'You're a snob,' he concludes.

'About some things, I suppose I am. Listen, Boyd, I'm working. I have to go.' Amelia hangs up the phone. She is not vain about her looks and she certainly doesn't value the opinion of Boyd Flanagan, who hadn't really been talking to her anyway. She is just his most recent disappointment. She has had disappointments, too.

She is thirty-one years old and she thinks she should have met someone by now.

And yet . . .

Amelia the bright-sider believes it is better to be alone than to be with someone who doesn't share your sensibilities and interests. (It *is*, right?)

Her mother likes to say that novels have ruined Amelia for real men. This observation insults Amelia because it implies that she only reads books with classically romantic heroes. She does not mind the occasional novel with a romantic hero but her reading tastes are far more varied than that. Furthermore, she adores Humbert Humbert as a character while accepting the fact that she wouldn't really want him for a life partner, a boyfriend, or even a casual acquaintance. She feels the same way about Holden Caulfield, and Misters Rochester and Darcy.

The sign over the porch of the purple Victorian cottage is faded, and Amelia nearly walks past it.

ISLAND BOOKS

Alice Island's Exclusive Provider
of Fine Literary Content since 1999
No Man Is an Island; Every Book Is a World

Inside, a teenager minds the till while reading the new Alice Munro collection. 'Oh, how is that one?' Amelia asks. Amelia adores Munro, but aside from vacation, she rarely has time to read books that aren't on the list.

'It's for school,' the girl replies, as if that settles the question.

Amelia introduces herself as the sales rep from Knightley Press, and the teenager, without looking up from the page, points vaguely to the back. 'A.J.'s in his office.'

Precarious stacks of Advance Reading Copies (ARCs) and galleys line the hallway, and Amelia feels the usual flash of despair. The tote bag that is embossing her shoulder has several additions for A.J.'s piles and a catalogue filled with other books for her to pitch. She never lies about the books on her list. She never says she loves a book if she doesn't. She can usually find something positive to say about a book or, failing that, the cover or, failing that, the author or, failing that, the author's website. *And that's why they pay me the big bucks*, Amelia occasionally jokes to herself. She makes $37,000 per year plus the possibility of bonuses, though no one who does her job has made a bonus for a very long time.

The door to A. J. Fikry's office is closed. Amelia is halfway to it when the sleeve of her sweater catches on one of the stacks, and one hundred books, maybe more, crash to the ground with a mortifying thunder. The door opens, and A. J. Fikry looks from the wreckage to the dirty-blond giantess, who is frantically trying to repile the books. 'Who the hell are you?'

'Amelia Loman.' She stacks ten more tomes and half of them tumble down.

'Leave it,' A.J. commands. 'There's an order to these things. You are not helping. Please leave.'

Amelia stands. She is at least four inches taller than A.J. 'But we have a meeting.'

'We have no meeting,' A.J. says.

'*We do*,' Amelia insists. 'I e-mailed you last week about the winter list. You said it was fine for me to come by either Thursday or Friday afternoon. I said I'd come on Thursday.'

The e-mail exchange had been brief, but she knows it was not fiction.

'You're a rep?'

Amelia nods, relieved.

'What publisher again?'

'Knightley.'

'Knightley Press is Harvey Rhodes,' A.J. replies. 'When you e-mailed me last week, I thought you were Harvey's assistant or something.'

'I'm Harvey's replacement.'

A.J. sighs heavily. 'What company has Harvey gone to?'

Harvey is dead, and for a second Amelia considers making a bad joke casting the afterlife as a sort of company and Harvey as an employee in it. 'He's dead,' she says flatly. 'I thought you would have heard.' Most of her accounts had already heard. Harvey had been a legend, as much as a sales rep can be a legend. 'There was an obituary in the ABA newsletter and maybe one in *Publishers Weekly*, too,' she says by way of apology.

'I don't much follow publishing news,' A.J. says. He takes off his thick black glasses and then spends a long time wiping the frames.

'I'm sorry if it's a shock to you.' Amelia puts her hand on A.J.'s arm, and he shakes her off.

'What do I care? I barely knew the man. I saw him three times a year. Not enough to call him a friend. And every time I saw him, he was trying to sell me something. This is not friendship.'

Amelia can tell that A.J. is in no mood to be pitched the winter list. She should offer to come back some other day.

But then she thinks of the two-hour drive to Hyannis and the eighty-minute boat ride to Alice and the ferry schedule, which becomes more irregular after October. 'Since I'm here,' Amelia says, 'would you mind if we went through Knightley's winter titles?'

A.J.'s office is a closet. It has no windows, no pictures on the wall, no family photos on the desk, no knick-knacks, no escape. The office has books, inexpensive metal shelves like the kind for a garage, a filing cabinet and an ancient, possibly twentieth-century, desktop computer. A.J. does not offer her a drink, and although Amelia is thirsty, she doesn't ask for one. She clears a chair of books and sits.

Amelia launches into the winter list. It's the smallest list of the year, both in size and expectations. A few big (or at least promising) debuts, but other than that it is filled with the books for which the publisher has the lowest commercial hopes. Despite this, Amelia often likes the 'winters' the best. They are the underdogs, the sleepers, the long shots. (It is not too much of a stretch to point out that this is how she sees herself, too.) She leaves for last her favourite book, a memoir written by an eighty-year-old man, a life-long bachelor who married at the age of seventy-eight. His bride died two years after the wedding at the age of eighty-three. Cancer. According to his bio, the writer worked as a science reporter for various midwestern newspapers, and the prose is precise, funny, not at all maudlin. Amelia had cried uncontrollably on the train from New York to Providence. Amelia knows *The Late Bloomer* is a small book and that the description sounds more than a little clichéd, but she feels sure other people will love it if they give it a chance. In Amelia's experience, most people's problems would be solved if they would only give more things a chance.

Amelia is halfway through describing *The Late Bloomer* when A.J. puts his head on the desk.

'Is something wrong?' Amelia asks.

'This is not for me,' A.J. says.

'Just try the first chapter.' Amelia is pushing the galley into his hand. 'I know the subject matter could be incredibly corny, but when you see how it's writ—'

He cuts her off. 'This is not for me.'

'Okay, so I'll tell you about something else.'

A.J. takes a deep breath. 'You seem like a nice enough young woman, but your predecessor … The thing is, Harvey knew my tastes. He had the same taste as me.'

Amelia sets the galley on the desk. 'I'd like the chance to get to know your tastes,' she says, feeling a bit like a character in a porno.

He mutters something under his breath. She thinks it sounds like *What's the point?* but she isn't sure.

Amelia closes the Knightley catalogue. 'Mr Fikry, please just tell me what you like.'

'*Like*,' he repeats with distaste. 'How about I tell you what I don't like? I do not like postmodernism, post-apocalyptic settings, post-mortem narrators or magic realism. I rarely respond to supposedly clever formal devices, multiple fonts, pictures where they shouldn't be – basically, gimmicks of any kind. I find literary fiction about the Holocaust or any other major world tragedy to be distasteful – non-fiction only, please. I do not like genre mash-ups à la the literary detective novel or the literary fantasy. Literary should be literary, and genre should be genre, and crossbreeding rarely results in anything satisfying. I do not like children's books, especially ones with orphans, and I prefer not to clutter my shelves with young adult. I do not like anything over four hundred pages or under one hundred fifty pages. I am repulsed by ghostwritten novels by reality television stars, celebrity picture books, sports memoirs, movie tie-in editions, novelty items and – I imagine this goes without saying – vampires. I rarely stock debuts, chick lit, poetry or translations. I would prefer not to stock series, but the demands of my pocketbook require me to. For your part, you needn't tell me about the "next big series" until it is ensconced on the *New York Times* Best Sellers list. Above all, Ms Loman, I find slim literary memoirs about little old men whose little old wives have died from cancer to be absolutely intolerable. No matter how well written the sales rep claims they are. No matter how many copies you promise I'll sell on Mother's Day.'

Amelia blushes, though she is angry more than embarrassed. She agrees with some of what A.J. has said, but his manner is unnecessarily insulting. Knightley Press doesn't even sell half of that stuff anyway. She studies him. He is older than Amelia but not by much, not by more than ten years. He is too young to like so little. 'What *do* you like?' she asks.

'Everything else,' he says. 'I will also admit to an occasional weakness for short-story collections. Customers never want to buy them though.'

There is only one short-story collection on Amelia's list,

a debut. Amelia hasn't read the whole thing, and time dictates that she probably won't, but she liked the first story. An American sixth-grade class and an Indian sixth-grade class participate in an international pen-pal programme. The narrator is an Indian kid in the American class who keeps feeding comical misinformation about Indian culture to the Americans. She clears her throat, which is still terribly dry. '*The Year Bombay Became Mumbai*. I think it will have special int—'

'No,' he says.

'I haven't even told you what it's about yet.'

'Just no.'

'But why?'

'If you're honest with yourself, you'll admit that you're only telling me about it because I'm partially Indian and you think this will be my special interest. Am I right?'

Amelia imagines smashing the ancient computer over his head. 'I'm telling you about this because you said you liked short stories! And it's the only one on my list. And for the record' – here, she lies – 'it's completely wonderful from start to finish. Even if it is a debut.

'And do you know what else? I love debuts. I love discovering something new. It's part of the whole reason I do this job.' Amelia rises. Her head is pounding. Maybe she does drink too much? Her head is pounding and her heart is, too. 'Do you want my opinion?'

'Not particularly,' he says. 'What are you, twenty-five?'

'Mr Fikry, this is a lovely store, but if you continue in this this this' – as a child, she stuttered and it occasionally returns when she is upset; she clears her throat – 'this backward way of thinking, there won't be an Island Books before too long.'

Amelia sets *The Late Bloomer* along with the winter catalogue on his desk. She trips over the books in the hallway as she leaves.

The next ferry doesn't depart for another hour so she takes her time walking back through town. Outside a Bank of America, a bronze plaque commemorates the summer Herman Melville had spent there, back when the building had been the Alice Inn. She holds out her phone and takes a picture of herself with the plaque. Alice is a nice enough place, but she imagines she won't have reason to be back anytime soon.

She texts her boss in New York: *Doesn't look like there'll be any orders from Island.* ☹

The boss replies: *Don't fret. Only a little account, and Island does the bulk of its ordering in anticipation of the summer when the tourists are there. The guy who runs the place is weird, and Harvey always had better luck selling the spring/summer list. You will, too.*

At six o'clock, A.J. tells Molly Klock to leave. 'How's the new Munro?' he asks.

She groans. 'Why does everyone keep asking me that today?' She is only referring to Amelia, but Molly likes to speak in extremes.

'I suppose because you're reading it.'

Molly groans again. 'Okay. The people are, I dunno, too human sometimes.'

'I think that's rather the point with Munro,' he says.

'Dunno. Prefer the old stuff. See you on Monday.'

Something will have to be done about Molly, A.J. thinks as he flips the sign to CLOSED. Aside from liking to read, Molly is truly a terrible bookseller. But she's only a part-timer, and it's such a bother to train someone new, and at least she doesn't steal. Nic had hired her so she must have seen something in the surly Miss Klock. Maybe next summer A.J. will work up the energy to fire Molly.

A.J. kicks the remaining customers out (he is most annoyed by an organic chemistry study group who have bought nothing but have been camped out in magazines since four – he's pretty sure one of them clogged up the toilet, too), then deals with the receipts, a task as depressing as it sounds. Finally, he goes upstairs to the attic apartment where he lives. He pops a carton of frozen vindaloo into the microwave. Nine minutes, per the box's instructions. As he's standing there, he thinks of the girl from Knightley. She had looked like a time traveller from 1990s Seattle with her anchor-printed galoshes and her floral grandma dress and her fuzzy beige sweater and her shoulder-length hair that looked like it had been cut in the kitchen by her boyfriend. Girlfriend? Boyfriend, he decides. He thinks of Courtney Love when she was married to Kurt Cobain. The tough rose mouth says *No one can hurt me,* but the soft blue eyes say *Yes you can and you probably will.* And he had made that big dandelion of a girl cry. *Well done, A.J.*

The scent of vindaloo is growing stronger, but seven and a half minutes remain on the clock.

He wants a task. Something physical but not strenuous.

He goes into the basement to collapse book boxes with his box cutter. Knife. Flatten. Stack. Knife. Flatten. Stack.

A.J. regrets his behaviour with the rep. It hadn't been her fault. Someone should have told him that Harvey Rhodes had died.

Knife. Flatten. Stack.

Someone probably *had* told him. A.J. only skims his e-mail, never answers his phone. Had there been a funeral? Not that A.J. would have attended anyway. He had barely known Harvey Rhodes. *Obviously.*

Knife. Flatten. Stack.

And yet ... He had spent hours with the man over the last half-dozen years. They had only ever discussed books but what, in this life, is more personal than books?

Knife. Flatten. Stack.

And how rare is it to find someone who shares your tastes? The one real fight they'd ever had was over David Foster Wallace. It was around the time of Wallace's suicide. A.J. had found the reverent tone of the eulogies to be insufferable. The man had written a decent (if indulgent and overlong) novel, a few modestly insightful essays and not much else.

'*Infinite Jest* is a masterpiece,' Harvey had said.

'*Infinite Jest* is an endurance contest. You manage to get through it and you have no choice but to say you like it. Otherwise, you have to deal with the fact that you just wasted weeks of your life,' A.J. had countered. 'Style, no substance, my friend.'

Harvey's face had reddened as he leaned over the desk. 'You say that about any writer who was born in the same decade as you!'

Knife. Flatten. Stack. Tie.

By the time he gets back upstairs, the vindaloo is cold again. If he reheats it in that plastic dish, he'll probably end up with cancer.

He takes the plastic tray to the table. The first bite is burning. The second bite is frozen. Papa Bear's vindaloo and Baby Bear's vindaloo. He throws the tray against the wall. How little he had meant to Harvey and how much Harvey had meant to him.

The difficulty of living alone is that any mess he makes he is forced to clean up himself.

No, the real difficulty of living alone is that no one cares if you are upset. No one cares why a thirty-nine-year-old man has thrown a plastic tub of vindaloo across a room like a toddler. He pours himself a glass of Merlot. He spreads a tablecloth on the table. He walks into the living room. He unlocks a climate-controlled glass case and removes *Tamerlane* from it. Back in the kitchen, he sets *Tamerlane* across the table from him, props it against the chair where Nic used to sit.

'Cheers, you piece of crap,' he says to the slim volume.

He finishes the glass. He pours himself another, and after he finishes that he promises himself that he's going to read a book. Maybe an old favourite like *Old School* by Tobias Wolff, though his time would certainly be better spent on something new. What had that dopey rep been going on about? *The Late Bloomer* – ugh. He had meant what he said. There is nothing worse than cutesy memoirs about widowers. Especially if one is a widower as A.J. has been for the last twenty-one months. The rep had been new – not her fault that she didn't know about his boring

personal tragedy. God, he misses Nic. Her voice and her
neck and even her <u>armpits</u>. They had been stubbly as a
cat's tongue and, at the end of the day, smelled like milk
just before it curdles.

Three glasses later, he passes out at the table. He is only
five foot seven inches tall, 140 pounds, and he hasn't even
had frozen vindaloo to <u>fortify</u> him. No dent will be made in
his reading pile tonight.

'Ajay,' Nic whispers. 'Go to bed.'

At last, he is dreaming. The point of all the drinking is
to arrive in this place.

Nic, his drunken-dream ghost wife, helps him to his
feet.

'You're a disgrace, nerd. You know that?'

He nods.

'Frozen vindaloo and five-dollar red wine.'

'I am respecting the time-honoured traditions of my
<u>heritage</u>.'

He and the ghost shuffle to the bedroom.

'Congratulations, Mr Fikry. You're turning into a bona
fide alcoholic.'

'I'm sorry,' he says. She lowers him into the bed.

Her brown hair is short, gamine-style. 'You cut your
hair,' he says. 'Weird.'

'You were awful to that girl today.'

'It was about Harvey.'

'Obviously,' she says.

'I don't like it when people who used to know you die.'

'That's why you won't fire Molly Klock, too?'

He nods.

'You can't go on like this.'

'I can,' A.J. says. 'I have been. I will.'

She kisses him on the forehead. 'I guess what I'm saying is I don't want you to.'

She is gone.

The accident hadn't been anyone's fault. She'd been driving an author home after an afternoon event. She'd probably been speeding to catch the last automobile ferry back to Alice. Possibly she had swerved to avoid hitting a deer. Possibly Massachusetts roads in winter. There was no way to know. The cop at the hospital asked if she'd been suicidal. 'No,' A.J. said. 'Nothing like that.' She had been two months pregnant. They hadn't told anyone yet. There had been disappointments before. Standing in the waiting room outside the morgue, he rather wished they *had* told people. At least there would have been a brief period of happiness before this longer period of ... He did not yet know what to call *this*. 'No, she was not suicidal.' A.J. paused. 'She was a terrible driver who thought she wasn't.'

'Yes,' said the cop. 'It wasn't anyone's fault.'

'People like to say that,' A.J. replies. 'But it *was* someone's fault. It was hers. What a stupid thing for her to do. What a stupid melodramatic thing for her to do. What a goddamn Danielle Steel move, Nic! If this were a novel, I'd stop reading right now. I'd throw it across the room.'

The cop (who was not much of a reader aside from the occasional Jeffery Deaver mass-market paperback while on vacation) tried to steer the conversation back to reality. 'That's right. You own the bookstore.'

'My wife and I,' A.J. replied without thinking. 'Oh Christ, I just did that stupid thing where the character forgets that the spouse has died and he accidentally uses "we". That's such a cliché. Officer' – he paused to read the cop's badge – 'Lambiase, you and I are characters in a bad novel. Do you know that? How the heck did we end up here? You're probably thinking to yourself, *Poor bastard*, and tonight you'll hug your kids extra tight because that's what characters in these kinds of novels do. You know the kind of book I'm talking about, right? The kind of hotshot literary fiction that, like, follows some unimportant supporting character for a bit so it looks all Faulkneresque and expansive. Look how the author cares for the little people! The common man! How broad-minded he or she must be! Even your name. Officer Lambiase is the perfect name for a clichéd Massachusetts cop. Are you racist, Lambiase? Because your kind of character ought to be racist.'

'Mr Fikry,' Officer Lambiase had said. 'Is there anyone I can call for you?' He was a good cop, accustomed to the many ways the aggrieved can come undone. He set his hand on A.J.'s shoulder.

'Yes! Right on, Officer Lambiase, that's exactly what you're supposed to do in this moment! You're playing your part beautifully. Would you happen to know what the widower is supposed to do next?'

'Call someone,' Officer Lambiase said.

'Yes, that is probably right. I've already called my in-laws, though.' A.J. nodded. 'If this were a short story, you and I would be done by now. A small ironic turn and out. That's why there's nothing more elegant in the prose universe than a short story, Officer Lambiase.

'If this were Raymond Carver, you'd offer me some meagre comfort and darkness would set in and all this would be over. But this . . . is feeling more like a novel to me after all. Emotionally, I mean. It will take me a while to get through it. Do you know?'

'I'm not sure that I do. I haven't read Raymond Carver,' Officer Lambiase said. 'I like Lincoln Rhyme. Do you know him?'

'The quadriplegic criminologist. Decent for genre writing. But have you read any short stories?' A.J. asked.

'Maybe in school. Fairy tales. Or, um, *The Red Pony*? I think I was supposed to read *The Red Pony*.'

'*That* is a novella,' A.J. said.

'Oh, sorry. I'm . . . Wait, there was one with a cop I remember from high school. Kind of a perfect crime thing, which I guess is why I remember it. This cop gets killed by his wife. The weapon is a frozen side of beef and then she serves it to the other—'

'"Lamb to the Slaughter".' A.J. said. 'The story's called "Lamb to the Slaughter" and the weapon is a leg of lamb.'

'Yes, that's it!' The cop was delighted. 'You know your stuff.'

'It's a very well-known piece,' A.J. said. 'My in-laws should be here any minute. I'm sorry about before when I referred to you as an "unimportant supporting character". That was rude and for all we know, I am the "unimportant

supporting character" in the grander saga of Officer
Lambiase. A cop is a more likely protagonist than a bookseller. You, sir, are a genre.'

'Hmmm,' said Officer Lambiase. 'You're probably right
at that. Going back to what we were talking about before.
As a cop, my problem with the story is the timeline. Like,
she puts the beef—'

'Lamb.'

'Lamb. So she kills the guy with the frozen lamb chop
then she puts it in the oven to cook without even <u>thawing</u>
it. I'm no Rachael Ray, but . . . '

Nic had begun to freeze by the time they had pulled her
car out of the water, and in the morgue drawer her lips had
been blue. The colour had reminded A.J. of the black lipstick she'd worn to the book party she'd thrown for the
latest vampire whatever. He hadn't cared for the idea of
silly teenage girls prancing about Island in prom dresses,
but Nic, who had actually *liked* that damned vampire book
and the woman who wrote it, insisted that a vampire prom
was good for business and also fun. 'You remember fun,
right?'

'<u>Dimly</u>,' he had said. 'Long ago, back before I was a
bookseller, back when I had my weekends and my nights to
myself, back when I read for pleasure, I recall that there was
fun. So, dimly, dimly. Yes.'

'Let me refresh your memory. Fun is having a smart,
pretty, easy wife with whom you get to spend every working day.'

He could still picture her in that ridiculous black satin
dress, her right arm draped around the porch column and

her comely stained lips in a line. 'Tragically, my wife has been turned into a vampire.'

'You poor man.' She crossed the porch and kissed him, leaving a lipstick trace like a bruise. 'Your only move is to become a vampire, too. Don't try to fight it. That's the absolute worst thing you could do. You gotta be cool, nerd. Invite me in.'

The Diamond as Big as the Ritz

1922/F. Scott Fitzgerald

Technically, a novella. But then novella is something of a grey area. Still, if you find yourself among the kind of people who bother to make such distinctions – and I used to be that type of person – it is best that you know the difference. (If you end up going to an Ivy League college,* you are likely to run into such people. Arm yourself with knowledge against this bumptious lot. But I digress.) E. A. Poe defines a short story as readable in a single sitting. I imagine a 'single sitting' was longer back in his day. But I digress again.

Gimmicky, oddball story of the challenges of owning a town made of diamonds and of the lengths the rich will go to protect their way of life. Fitzgerald is in fine form here. The Great Gatsby *is unquestionably dazzling, but that novel occasionally seems overgroomed to me, like a garden topiary. The short-story format is a roomier, messier affair for him. 'Diamond' breathes like an enchanted garden gnome.*

* *I have thoughts about this. Remember that a fine education can be found in places other than the usual.*

*Re: its inclusion. Shall I do the obvious thing and tell you that
just before I met you I too lost something of great, if speculative,
value?*

— A.J.F.

Though he can't remember how he got there or having taken off his clothes, A.J. wakes in bed wearing only his underwear. He remembers that Harvey Rhodes is dead; he remembers being an asshole to the comely Knightley Press rep; he remembers throwing the vindaloo across the room; he remembers the first glass of wine and the toast to *Tamerlane*. After that, oblivion. From his point of view, the evening had been a triumph.

His head is pounding. He walks out to the main room, expecting to find the vindaloo detritus. The floor and the walls are spotless. A.J. digs an aspirin out of the cabinet while silently congratulating himself for having had the foresight to clean up the vindaloo. He sits down at the dining-room table and notices that the wine bottle has also been thrown out. Odd for him to have been so fastidious but not unprecedented. He is nothing if not a neat drunk. He looks across the table to where he'd left *Tamerlane*. The book is gone. Maybe he only *thought* he'd taken it out of the case?

As he walks across the room, A.J.'s heart is pounding in competition with his head. Halfway to the bookcase, he can see that the combination-locked, climate-controlled glass coffin, which protects *Tamerlane* from the world, is wide open and empty.

He pulls on a bathrobe and throws on his running shoes, which haven't gotten much mileage on them of late.

A.J. jogs down Captain Wiggins Street with his dingy plaid bathrobe flapping out behind him. He looks like a depressed, malnourished superhero. He turns onto Main and runs straight into the sleepy Alice Island Police Station. 'I've been robbed!' A.J. announces. It was only a short run, but A.J. is breathing hard. 'Please, someone help me!' He tries not to feel like an old lady with a stolen handbag.

Lambiase sets down his cup of coffee and takes in the distraught man in the bathrobe. He recognizes him as the owner of the bookstore and the man whose pretty young wife had driven into the lake a year and a half back. A.J. looks much older than the last time he'd seen him, though Lambiase supposes that is to be expected.

'All right, Mr Fikry,' Lambiase says, 'tell me what happened.'

'Someone stole *Tamerlane*,' A.J. says.

'What's *Tamerlane*?'

'It's a book. It's a very valuable book.'

'To clarify. You mean someone *shoplifted* a book from the store.'

'No. It was *my* book from my personal collection. It is an extremely rare collection of poems by Edgar Allan Poe.'

'So, it's, like, your favourite book?' Lambiase asks.

'No. I don't even like it. It's crap, it's jejune crap. It's . . .' A.J. is hyperventilating. 'Fuck.'

'Calm down, Mr Fikry. I'm trying to understand. You don't like the book, but it has sentimental value?'

'No! Fuck sentimental value. It has great financial value.

Tamerlane is like the Honus Wagner of rare books! You know what I'm saying?'

'Sure, my pops was a baseball card collector.' Lambiase nods. 'That valuable?'

A.J. can't get the words out fast enough. 'It was the first thing Edgar Allan Poe ever wrote, back when he was eighteen. Copies are extremely rare because the print run was fifty copies, and it was published anonymously. Instead of "by Edgar Allan Poe", it says "by a Bostonian" on the cover. Copies sell for upward of four hundred thousand dollars depending on condition and the mood of the rare-books market. I was planning to auction it off in a couple of years when the economy had had a little time to improve. I was planning to close the shop and retire on the proceeds.'

'If you don't mind my asking,' Lambiase says, 'why would you keep something like that in your house and not in a bank vault?'

A.J. shakes his head. 'I don't know. I was stupid. I liked keeping it close by, I suppose. I liked being able to look at it and be reminded that I could quit any time I wanted to. I kept it in a combination-locked glass case. I thought it was safe enough.' In his defence, there is very little theft in Alice Island except during tourist season. It is October.

'So, did someone break the case or did someone know the combination?' Lambiase asks.

'Neither. I wanted to get wasted last night. Fucking stupid, but I took out the book so I could look at it. A poor excuse for company, I know.'

'Mr Fikry, was *Tamerlane* insured?'

A.J. puts his head in his hands. Lambiase takes that to mean that the book wasn't. 'I only found the book about a year ago, a couple of months after my wife died. I didn't want to spend the extra money. I never got around to it. I don't know. A million retrospectively idiotic reasons, the main one being that I am an idiot, Officer Lambiase.'

Lambiase doesn't bother telling him that it is *Chief* Lambiase. 'Here's what I'm gonna do. First, you and me are gonna file a police report. Then, when my detective comes in – she's only on half days during the off-season – I'm gonna send her down to your place to look for finger-prints and other evidence. Maybe something'll come up. The other thing we can do is call the auction houses and other people who deal in these sorts of items. If it's as rare a book as you say, people will notice if an unaccounted-for copy comes on the market. Don't things like that need to have a record of who owned them, a whatchamacallit?'

'A provenance,' A.J. says.

'Yeah, exactly! My wife used to watch *Antiques Roadshow*. You ever seen that show?'

A.J. doesn't reply.

'One last thing, I'm wondering who knew about the book?'

A.J. snorts. 'Everyone. My wife's sister, Ismay, teaches at the high school. She worries about me since Nic . . . She's always bugging me to get out of the store, get off the island. About a year ago, she dragged me to this dreary estate sale in Milton. It was sitting in a box with about fifty other books, all worthless except *Tamerlane*. I paid five dollars. The people had no idea what they had. I felt kind of shitty about taking it, if you want to know the truth. Not that it matters now. Anyway, Ismay thought it would be good for business and educational or some crap if I put it on display in the store. So I kept the case in the shop all last summer. You never come to the store, I guess.'

Lambiase looks at his shoes, the familiar shame of a thousand high school English classes where he'd failed to do the minimum required reading rushing back to him. 'Not much of a reader.'

'You read some crime, though, right?'

'Good memory,' Lambiase says. In fact, A.J. has a perfect memory for people's reading tastes.

'Deaver, was it? If you like that, there's this new writer from—'

'Sure, I'll stop by sometime. Is there someone I can call for you? Your wife's sister is Ismay Evans-Parish, right?'

'Ismay's at—' At that moment, A.J. freezes as if someone has pressed the pause button on him. His eyes are blank and his mouth drops open.

'Mr Fikry?'

For nearly thirty seconds, A.J. is frozen and then he resumes speaking as if nothing has happened. 'Ismay's at work, and I'm fine. There's no need to call her.'

'You were gone for a minute there,' Lambiase says.

'What?'

'You blacked out.'

'Oh Christ. It's just an *absence* seizure. I used to have them a lot as a kid. I rarely have them as an adult except when I'm unusually stressed.'

'You should see a doctor.'

'No, it's fine. Honestly. I just want to find my book.'

'I'd feel better,' Lambiase insists. 'You've had a pretty traumatic morning, and I know you live alone. I'm gonna take you to the hospital and then I'm gonna have your in-laws meet you there. Meanwhile, I'll have my guys see if they can figure anything out about your book.'

At the hospital, A.J. waits, fills out forms, waits, strips, waits, takes tests, waits, puts his clothes back on, waits, takes more tests, waits, strips again, and at last is seen by a middle-aged general practitioner. She is not particularly concerned about the seizure. The tests, however, have revealed that his blood pressure and cholesterol are on the border between acceptable and high for a thirty-nine-year-old man. She asks A.J. about his lifestyle. He answers the question truthfully. 'I'm not what you'd call an alcoholic, but I do like to drink until I pass out at least once a week. I smoke occasionally and I subsist on a diet of frozen entrées. I rarely floss. I used to be a long-distance runner, but now I don't exercise at all. I live alone and I lack meaningful personal relationships. Since my wife died, I hate my work, too.'

'Oh, is that all?' the doctor asks. 'You're still a young man, Mr Fikry, but a body can only take so much. If you're trying to kill yourself, I can certainly think of faster, easier ways to go about it. Do you want to die?'

A response doesn't immediately occur to him.

'Because if you really want to die, I can put you under psychiatric observation.'

'I don't want to die,' A.J. says after a bit. 'I just find it dif-ficult to be *here* all the time. Do you think I'm crazy?'

'No. I can see why you would feel that way. You're going through a bear of a time. Start with exercise,' she says. 'You'll feel better.'

'Okay.'

'Your wife was lovely,' the doctor says. 'I used to be in the mother–daughter book club she ran at the store. My daughter still works for you part-time.'

'Molly Klock?'

'Klock is my partner's name. I'm Dr Rosen.' She taps her name tag.

In the lobby, A.J. encounters a familiar scene. 'Would you mind terribly?' a nurse in pink scrubs asks, holding out a battered mass-market paperback to a man in a corduroy jacket with patches on the elbows.

'I'd be delighted,' Daniel Parish says. 'What's your name?'

'Jill, like Jack and Jill went up the hill. Macy, like the store. I've read all your books, but I like this one the best. Like, by far.'

'*That* is the popular opinion, Jill from the hill.' Daniel isn't kidding. None of his books have sold nearly as well as the first.

'I can't even express how much it meant to me. Like, I start to tear up thinking about it.' She bows her head and lowers her eyes, deferential as a geisha. 'It's what made me want to be a nurse! I just started working here. When I found out you lived in town, I kept hoping you'd come in some day.'

'You mean, you hoped I'd get sick?' Daniel says, smiling.

'No, of course not!' She blushes, then swats him on the arm. 'You! You're terrible!'

'I am,' Daniel replies. 'I am, indeed, terrible.'

The first time Nic had met Daniel Parish, she had commented that he had the good looks of an anchorman for a local news station. By the car ride home, she had revised her opinion. 'His eyes are too small for an anchor. He'd be the weatherman.'

'He does have a sonorous voice,' A.J. had said.

'If that man told you that the storm had passed, you would definitely believe him. Probably even if you were still standing smack in the middle of it,' she had said.

A.J. interrupts the flirtation. 'Dan,' he says. 'I thought they'd called *your wife*.' A.J. is not going for subtle.

Daniel clears his throat. 'She's feeling under the weather, so I came instead. How you holding up, old man?' Daniel calls A.J. 'old man' despite the fact that Daniel is five years older than A.J.

'I've lost my fortune, and the doctor says I'm going to die, but other than that, I'm fantastic.' The sedative has given him perspective.

'Great. Let's get drinks.' Daniel turns to Nurse Jill and whispers something in her ear. When Daniel returns the book to her, A.J. can see that he has written his phone number. 'Come, thou monarch of the vine!' Daniel says as he heads for the exit.

Despite the fact that he loves books and owns a bookstore, A.J. does not particularly care for writers. He finds them to be unkempt, narcissistic, silly and generally unpleasant people. He tries to avoid meeting the ones who've written books he loves for fear that they will ruin their books for him. Luckily, he does not love Daniel's books, not even the popular first novel. As for the man? Well, he amuses A.J. to an extent. This is to say, Daniel Parish is one of A.J.'s closest friends.

'It's my own fault,' A.J. says after his second beer. 'Should have gotten insurance. Should have stored it in a safe. Shouldn't have taken it out when I was drunk. No matter who stole it, I can't say my conduct was exactly faultless.' The alcohol in combination with the sedative is mellowing A.J., making him philosophical. Daniel pours him another glass from the pitcher.

'Don't do that, A.J. Don't blame yourself,' Daniel says.

'It's a wake-up call is what it is,' A.J. says. 'I'm definitely gonna cut down on my drinking.'

'Right after this beer,' Daniel quips. They clink mugs. A high school girl in denim cut-offs so short her buttocks peek out the bottom walks into the bar. Daniel holds up his mug to her. 'Nice outfit!' The girl gives him the finger. 'You gotta stop drinking. I gotta stop cheating on Ismay,' Daniel says. 'But then I see a pair of shorts like that, and my resolve is seriously tested. This night's been ridiculous. The nurse! Those shorts!'

A.J. sips the beer. 'How's the book coming?'

Daniel shrugs. 'It is a book. It will have pages and a cover. It will have a plot, characters, complications. It will reflect years of studying, refining and practising my craft. For all that, it will surely be less popular than the first one I wrote at the age of twenty-five.'

'Poor bastard,' A.J. says.

'I'm pretty sure *you* win the Poor Bastard of the Year Award, old man.'

'Lucky me.'

'Poe's a lousy writer, you know? And *Tamerlane* is the worst. Boring Lord Byron rip-off. It'd be one thing if it were a first edition of something fucking decent. You should be glad to be rid of it. I loathe collectable books anyway. People getting all moony over particular paper carcasses. It's the ideas that matter, man. The words,' Daniel Parish says.

A.J. finishes his beer. 'You, sir, are an idiot.'

The investigation lasts a month, which in Alice Island PD time is like a year. Lambiase and his team find no relevant physical evidence at the scene. In addition to throwing out the wine bottle and cleaning up the vindaloo, the criminal had apparently wiped down the apartment of fingerprints. The investigators question A.J.'s employees and also his few friends and relations in Alice. These interviews result in nothing particularly incriminating. No book dealers or auction houses report any copies of *Tamerlane* turning up either. (Of course, auction houses are notoriously quiet about these matters.) The investigation is considered unsolved. The book is gone, and A.J. knows he will never see it again.

The glass case, now, has no use, and A.J. is unsure of what to do with it. He has no other rare books. Still, the case had been pricey, nearly five hundred dollars. Some vestigial, hopeful part of him wants to believe that something better could come along to put in the case. When he bought it, he was told he could also use it to store cigars.

As retirement is no longer on the horizon, A.J. reads galleys, returns e-mails, answers the phone, and even writes a shelf talker or two. At night, after the store is closed, he starts running again. There are many challenges to long-distance running, but one of the greatest is the question of where to put one's house keys. In the end, A.J. decides to leave his front door unlocked. In his estimation, nothing here is worth stealing.

The Luck of Roaring Camp

1868/Bret Harte

Overly sentimental tale of a mining camp that adopts an 'Ingin baby' whom they dub Luck. I read it for the first time at Princeton in a seminar called the Literature of the American West and was not moved in the least. In my response paper (dated November 14, 1992), the only things I found to recommend it were the colourful character names: Stumpy, Kentuck, French Pete, Cherokee Sal, etc. I chanced upon 'The Luck of Roaring Camp' again a couple of years ago and I cried so much you'll find that my Dover Thrift Edition is waterlogged. Methinks I have grown soft in my middle age. But me also thinks my latter-day reaction speaks to the necessity of encountering stories at precisely the right time in our lives. Remember, Maya: the things we respond to at twenty are not necessarily the same things we will respond to at forty and vice versa. This is true in books and also in life.

— A.J.F.

I n the weeks after the robbery, Island Books experiences a slight but statistically improbable uptick in business. A.J. attributes the increase to the lesser-known economic indicator known as 'the Curious Townie'.

A well-meaning townie (W-MT) will sidle up to the desk. 'Any word on *Tamerlane*?' [Translation: *May I turn over your significant personal loss for my own amusement?*]

A.J. will reply, 'Nothing yet.' [Translation: *Life still ruined.*]

W-MT: Oh, I'm sure something will turn up. [Translation: *Since I have no investment in the outcome of this situation, it costs me nothing to be optimistic.*] What's new that I haven't read?

A.J.: We've got a couple things. [Translation: *Pretty much everything. You haven't been in here for months, possibly years.*]

W-MT: There was a book I read about in the *New York Times Book Review*. It had a red cover, maybe?

A.J.: Yeah, that sounds familiar. [Translation: *That is excessively vague. Author, title, description of the plot – these are more useful locators. That the cover might have been red and that it was in the* New York Times Book Review *helps me far less than you might think.*] Anything else you remember about it? [*Use your words.*]

A.J. will then lead the W-MT over to the new-release wall, where he makes sure to sell him or her a hardcover.

Strangely enough, Nic's death had had the opposite

effect on business. Though he had opened and closed the store with the emotionless regularity of an SS officer, the fiscal quarter after her death had posted the worst sales in Island's history. Of course, people had felt sorry for him then, but they had felt *too* sorry for him. Nic had been a local, one of their own. They had been touched when the Princeton graduate (and Alice Island High School salutatorian no less) had returned to Alice to open a bookstore with her serious-eyed husband. Refreshing to see a young person coming back home for a change. Once she died, they found they had nothing in common with A.J. except their shared loss of Nic. Did they blame him? Some of them did, a little. Why hadn't he been the one to drive that author home that night? They consoled themselves and whispered that he'd always been a little odd and – they swore they didn't mean this in a racist way – a little foreign; it's obvious the guy's not from around here, you know. (He was born in New Jersey.) They held their breath as they walked past the store, like it was a cemetery.

A.J. runs their credit cards and concludes that a theft is an acceptable social loss while a death is an isolating one. By December, sales have returned to their usual pre-theft rate.

Two Fridays before Christmas, two minutes before close, A.J. makes the rounds of kicking out and ringing up the last customers. A man in a puffy coat is hemming and hawing over the latest Alex Cross. 'Twenty-six dollars seems like a lot. You know I can get it cheaper online, right?' A.J. says that he does know as he shows the man the door. 'You should really lower your prices if you want to be competitive,' the man says.

'Lower my prices? *Lower. My. Prices.* I hadn't considered that before,' A.J. says mildly.

'Are you being cheeky, young man?'

'No, I'm thankful. And at the next Island Books shareholders' meeting, I'll definitely raise this innovative suggestion of yours. I know we want to remain competitive. Between you and me, for a time in the early oughties, we'd given up on competition. I thought it was a mistake, but my board decided that competition was best left to Olympic athletes, kids in spelling bees and cereal manufacturers. These days, I'm glad to report that we at Island Books are definitely in the competition business once again. The store's closed, by the way.' A.J. points toward the exit.

As puffy coat grumbles his way out the door, an old woman creaks over the threshold. She is a regular customer, so A.J. tries not to be too annoyed that she is coming in after hours. 'Ah, Mrs Cumberbatch,' he says. 'Unfortunately, we're closing now.'

'Mr Fikry, don't you turn those Omar Sharif eyes of yours on me. I am outraged at you.' Mrs Cumberbatch pushes past him and slams a plump paperback on the counter. 'The book you recommended to me yesterday is the worst book I have read in all my eighty-two years, and I would like my money back.'

A.J. looks from the book to the old woman. 'What was your problem with it?'

'*Problems*, Mr Fikry. To begin, it is narrated by Death! I am an eighty-two-year-old woman and I do not find it one bit pleasurable to read a five-hundred-fifty-two-page tome narrated by Death. I think it is a remarkably insensitive choice.'

A.J. apologizes but he is not sorry. Who are these people who think a book comes with a guarantee that they will like it? He processes the return. The book's spine is broken. He will not be able to resell it. 'Mrs Cumberbatch,' he cannot resist saying, 'it appears that you read this. I wonder how far along you got.'

'Yes, I read it,' she replies. 'I most certainly did read it. It kept me up all night, I was so angry with it. At this stage of my life, I would rather not be kept up all night. Nor do I wish to have my tears jerked at the rate at which this novel jerked them. The next time you recommend a book to me, I hope you'll keep that in mind, Mr Fikry.'

'I will,' he says. 'And I do apologize, Mrs Cumberbatch. Most of our customers have rather liked *The Book Thief*.'

Once the store is closed, A.J. goes upstairs to change into his running clothes. He leaves through the bookstore's front entrance and, as has become his custom, does not lock the door.

A.J. had run cross-country in his high school's team and then at Princeton. He picked up the sport mainly because he had no skill for any other sport aside from the close reading of texts. He never really considered running cross-country to be much of a talent. His high school coach had romantically referred to him as a reliable middleman, meaning that A.J. could be counted on to finish in the upper middle of any pack. Now that he hasn't run for a

while, he has to concede that it had been a talent. In his
current condition, he can't make it more than two miles
without stopping. He rarely runs more than five miles total,
and his back, legs and basically every part of him hurt. The
pain turns out to be a good thing. He used to pass his runs
by ruminating, and the pain distracts him from such a fruit-
less activity.

Toward the end of his run, snow begins to fall. Not
wanting to track mud indoors, A.J. stops on the porch to
take off his running shoes. He braces himself on the front
door, and it swings open. He knows that he didn't lock it,
but he is reasonably sure that he didn't leave it open. He
flips on the light. Nothing seems out of place. The cash
register doesn't look molested. Probably, the wind had
blown the door open. He flips off the light and is almost to
the stairs when he hears a cry, sharp like a bird. The cry
repeats, more insistent this time.

A.J. turns the lights back on. He walks back to the
entrance and then makes his way up and down each aisle
of the bookstore. He comes to the last row, the poorly
stocked Children's and Young Adult section. On the floor
sits a baby with the store's lone copy of *Where the Wild
Things Are* (one of the few picture books Island even deigns
to carry) in its lap and opened to the middle. It is a large
baby, A.J. thinks. Not a newborn. A.J. can't clock the age
because, aside from himself, he has never really known any
babies personally. He was an only child, and obviously, he
and Nic never had any of their own. The baby is wearing
a pink ski jacket. She has a full head of light brown, very
curly hair, cornflower-blue eyes and tan-coloured skin a

shade or two lighter than A.J.'s own. It's rather a pretty thing.

'Who the hell are you?' A.J. asks the baby.

For no apparent reason, she stops crying and smiles at him. 'Maya,' she answers.

That was easy, A.J. thinks. 'How old are you?' he asks.

Maya holds up two fingers.

'You're two?'

Maya smiles again and holds up her arms to him.

'Where is your mommy?'

Maya begins to cry. She continues to hold out her arms to A.J. Because he can't see his way to any other options, A.J. picks her up. She weighs at least as much as a twenty-four carton of hardcovers, heavy enough to strain his back. The baby puts her arms around his neck, and A.J. notes that she smells rather nice, like powder and baby oil. Clearly, this is not some neglected or abused infant. She is friendly, well dressed, and expects – nay, demands – affection. Surely the owner of this bundle will return at any moment with an explanation that makes perfect sense. A broken-down car, say? Or perhaps the mother was struck with a sudden case of food poisoning. In the future, he will rethink his unlocked-door policy. Though it had occurred to him that something might be stolen, he had never considered the possibility that something might be left.

She hugs him tighter. Over her shoulder, A.J. notices an Elmo doll sitting on the floor with a note attached to his matted red chest by a safety pin. He sets the baby down and picks up Elmo, a character A.J. has always despised because he seems too needy.

'Elmo!' Maya says.

'Yes,' A.J. says. 'Elmo.' He unpins the note and hands the baby the doll. The note reads:

To the Owner of This Bookstore:

This is Maya. She is twenty-five months old. She is VERY SMART, exceptionally verbal for her age, and a sweet, good girl. I want her to grow up to be a reader. I want her to grow up in a place with books and among people who care about those kinds of things. I love her very much, but I can no longer take care of her. The father cannot be in her life, and I do not have a family that can help. I am desperate.

Yours,

Maya's Mother

Fuck, A.J. thinks.

Maya cries again.

He picks up the baby. Her diaper is soiled. A.J. has never changed a diaper in his life though he is a modestly skilled gift wrapper. Back when Nic was alive, Island used to offer free gift wrap at Christmas, and he figures that diaper-changing and gift-wrapping must be related proficiencies. Next to the baby sits a bag, which A.J. sincerely hopes turns out to be a diaper bag. Thankfully, it is. He changes the baby on the floor of the store, trying not to dirty the rug or look at her private parts too much. The whole thing takes about twenty minutes. Babies move more than books and aren't as conveniently shaped. Maya watches him with a cocked head, pursed lips and a wrinkled nose.

A.J. apologizes. 'Sorry, Maya, but it wasn't exactly a pleasure cruise for me either. The quicker you stop shitting yourself, the quicker we don't have to do this.'

'Sorry,' she says. A.J. immediately feels awful.

'No, I'm sorry. I don't know anything about any of this. I'm an ass.'

'Ass!' she repeats, and then she giggles.

A.J. puts his running shoes back on, and then he hoists up the baby, the bag and the note, and heads for the police station.

Of course, Chief Lambiase would be on duty that night. It seems to be the man's lot to be present for the most important moments of A.J.'s life. A.J. presents the baby to the police officer. 'Someone left this in the store,' A.J. whispers so as not to wake Maya who has fallen asleep in his arms.

Lambiase is in the middle of eating a doughnut, an act he tries to hide because the cliché embarrasses him. Lambiase finishes chewing, then says to A.J. in a most unprofessional way, 'Aw, it likes you.'

'It's not my baby,' A.J. continues to whisper.

'Whose baby is it?'

'A customer's, I guess.' A.J. reaches into his pocket and hands Lambiase the note.

'Oh, wow,' Lambiase says. 'The mother left it for you.' Maya opens her eyes and smiles at Lambiase. 'Cute little thing, ain't she?' Lambiase leans over her, and the baby grabs his moustache. 'Who's got my moustache?' Lambiase says in a ridiculous baby voice. 'Who stole my moustache?'

'Chief Lambiase, I don't think you're showing an adequate amount of concern here.'

Lambiase clears his throat and straightens his back. 'Okay. Here's the thing. It's nine p.m. on a Friday. I'll place a call to the Department of Children and Families, but with the snow and the weekend and the ferry schedule, I doubt anyone will make it out here until Monday at the earliest. We'll try to track down the mother and also the father, just in case someone is looking for the little rascal.'

'Maya,' Maya says.

'Is that your name?' Lambiase says in his baby voice. 'It's a very good name.' Lambiase clears his throat again. 'Someone'll have to watch the kid over the weekend. I and some of the other cops could take turns doing it here, or—'

'No. It's fine,' A.J. says. 'Doesn't seem right to keep a baby in a police station.'

'Do you know anything about child care?' Lambiase asks.

'It's only for the weekend. How hard can it be? I'll call my sister-in-law. Anything she doesn't know, I'll Google.'

'Google,' the baby says.

'Google! That's a very big word! Ahem,' Lambiase says. 'Okay, I'll check back with you on Monday. Funny world, right? Someone steals a book from you; someone else leaves you a baby.'

'Ha,' says A.J.

By the time they arrive at the apartment, Maya is full-on crying, a sound somewhere between a New Year's Eve party horn and a fire alarm. A.J. deduces that she is hungry, but he has no clue what to feed a twenty-five-month-old. He pulls up her lip to see if she has teeth. She does and she uses them to try to bite him. He Googles the question: 'What do I feed a twenty-five-month-old?' and the answer that comes back is that most of them should be able to eat what their parents eat. What Google does not know is that most of what A.J. eats is disgusting. His fridge contains a variety of frozen foods, many of them spicy. He calls his sister-in-law Ismay for help.

'Sorry to bother you,' he says. 'But I was wondering what I should feed a twenty-five-month-old child?'

'Why were you wondering that?' Ismay asks in a tight voice.

He explains about someone having left the baby in the store, and after a pause Ismay says that she will be right over.

'Are you sure?' A.J. asks. Ismay is six months pregnant, and he doesn't want to disturb her.

'I'm sure. I'm glad you called. The Great American Novelist is out of town, and I've had insomnia these last couple of weeks anyway.'

Less than a half hour later, Ismay arrives with a bag of groceries from her kitchen: the makings of a salad, a tofu lasagne and half an apple crumble. 'The best I could do on short notice,' she says.

'No, it's perfect,' A.J. says. 'My kitchen is a fiasco.'

'Your kitchen is a crime scene,' she says.

When the baby sees Ismay, she bawls. 'She must miss her mother,' Ismay says. 'Maybe I remind her of her mother?' A.J. nods, though he thinks the real cause is that his sister-in-law frightens the baby. Ismay has stylishly cut, spiky red hair, pale skin and eyes, long, spindly limbs. All her features are a little too large, her gestures a little too animated. Pregnant, she is like a very pretty Gollum. Even her voice might be off-putting to a baby. It is precise, theatre-trained, always pitched to fill the room. In the fifteen or so years he has known her, A.J. thinks Ismay has aged like an actress should: from Juliet to Ophelia to Gertrude to Hecate.

Ismay warms up the food. 'Would you like me to feed her?' Ismay asks.

Maya eyes Ismay suspiciously. 'No, I'll give it a go,' A.J. says. He turns to Maya. 'Do you use utensils?'

Maya does not reply.

'You don't have a baby chair. You'll need to improvise a structure so she won't topple over,' Ismay says.

He sets Maya on the floor. He builds three walls out of a pile of galleys then lines the galley fort with bed pillows.

His first spoonful of lasagne goes in without any struggle. 'Easy,' he says.

The second spoonful, Maya turns her head at the last moment, sending sauce everywhere – on A.J., on the bed pillows, down the side of the galley fort. Maya turns back to him with a huge smile on her face, as if she has made the most fantastically clever joke.

'I hope you weren't planning to read those,' Ismay says.

After dinner, they put the baby to bed on the futon in the second bedroom.

'Why didn't you just leave the baby at the police station?' Ismay asks.

'Didn't seem right,' A.J. says.

'You're not thinking of keeping it, are you?' Ismay rubs her own belly.

'Of course not. I'm only watching it until Monday.'

'I suppose the mother could turn up by then, change her mind,' Ismay says.

A.J. hands Ismay the note to read.

'Poor thing,' Ismay says.

'I agree, but I couldn't do it. I couldn't abandon a child of mine in a bookstore.'

Ismay shrugs. 'The girl probably had her reasons.'

'How do you know that it's a girl?' A.J. asks. 'It could be a middle-aged woman at the end of her rope.'

'The voice of the letter sounds young to me, I guess. Maybe the handwriting, too,' Ismay says. She runs her fingers through her short hair. 'How are you holding up otherwise?'

'I'm okay,' A.J. says. He realizes that he hasn't thought about *Tamerlane* or Nic for hours.

Ismay washes the dishes even though A.J. tells her to leave it. 'I'm not going to keep her,' A.J. repeats. 'I live alone. I don't have much money saved, and business isn't exactly booming.'

'Of course not,' Ismay says. 'It wouldn't make sense with your lifestyle.' She dries the dishes then puts them away. 'It wouldn't hurt you to start eating the occasional fresh vegetable, however.'

Ismay kisses him on the cheek. A.J. thinks that she is so

like Nic but so unlike her. Sometimes the like parts (the face, the figure) seem hardest for him to bear; sometimes the unlike parts (the brain, the heart) do. 'Let me know if you need more help,' Ismay says.

Although Nic had been the younger sister, she had always worried about Ismay. From Nic's point of view, her older sister had been a primer on how not to live her life. Ismay had chosen a college because she had liked the pictures in the brochure, had married a man because he looked splendid in a tuxedo, and had started teaching because she'd seen a movie about an inspirational teacher. 'Poor Ismay,' Nic had said. 'She always ends up so disappointed.'

Nic would want me to be nicer to her sister, he thinks. 'How's the production coming?' A.J. asks.

Ismay smiles, and she looks like a little girl. 'My word, A.J., I wasn't aware that you even knew that there was one.'

'*The Crucible*,' A.J. says. 'Kids come into the store to buy copies.'

'Yes, that makes sense. Awful play, really. But the girls get to do a lot of screaming and yelling, which they enjoy. Me, less so. I always come to rehearsal with a bottle of Tylenol. And maybe in the midst of all that screaming and yelling, they accidentally learn a little about American history. Of course, the real reason I picked it is because there are so many female roles – less tears when I post the list, you know. But now, with the baby coming, it's starting to seem like, well, a *lot* of drama.'

Because he feels obligated to her for coming over with the food, A.J. volunteers to help. 'Maybe I could paint flats or print programmes or something?'

She wants to say, *How unlike you*, but she resists. Aside from her husband, she believes her brother-in-law to be one of the most selfish and self-centred men she has ever met. If one afternoon with a baby can have such a refining influence on A.J., imagine what could happen to Daniel when the baby is born. Her brother-in-law's small gesture gives her hope. She rubs her belly. It's a boy in there, and they've already chosen a name and a back-up name if the original name doesn't suit.

The next afternoon, once the snow has stopped and even begun to melt away into mud, a body washes up against the small strip of land near the lighthouse. The ID in her pocket says that this is Marian Wallace, and it does not take long for Lambiase to deduce that the body and the baby are, in fact, related.

Marian Wallace has no people on Alice, and no one knows why she was here or who she came to see or why she decided to kill herself by swimming into the icy waters of the Alice Island Sound in December. That is to say, no one knows the specific reason. They know that Marian Wallace is black, that she is twenty-two years old and that she had a twenty-five-month-old toddler. To these facts they can add what she wrote in her note to A.J. A flawed but adequate narrative emerges. Law enforcement concludes that Marian Wallace is a suicide, nothing more.

As the weekend goes on, more information about Marian Wallace emerges. She attended Harvard on a scholarship. She was a Massachusetts State Champion swimmer and an avid creative writer. She was from Roxbury. Her mother is dead – cancer when Marian was thirteen. The maternal grandmother died a year later of the same cause. Her father is a drug addict. She spent her high school years in and out of foster care. One of her foster mothers remembers young Marian always with her head in a book. No one knows who the father of her baby is. No one even remembers her having a boyfriend. She was put on academic leave from college because she failed all her classes the previous semester – the demands of motherhood and a rigorous academic schedule having become too much to bear. She was pretty and smart, which makes her death a tragedy. She was poor and black, which means people say they saw it coming.

Sunday night, Lambiase stops by the bookstore to check on Maya and give A.J. the update. He has several younger siblings and he offers to watch Maya while A.J. tends to store business. 'Do you mind?' A.J. asks. 'Don't you have somewhere to go?'

Lambiase is recently divorced. He had married his high school sweetheart, so it took him a long time to realize that she was not, in fact, a sweetheart or a very nice person at all. In arguments, she was fond of calling him stupid and fat. He is not stupid, by the way, though he is neither well read nor well travelled. He is not fat, though he is built like a bulldog – thick-muscled neck, short legs, broad, flat nose. A sturdy American bulldog, not an English one.

Lambiase does not miss his wife, though he does miss having somewhere to go after work.

He parks himself on the floor and pulls Maya onto his

lap. After Maya falls asleep, Lambiase tells A.J. the things he's learned about the mother.

'What's strange to me,' A.J. says, 'is why she was on Alice Island in the first place. It's kind of a pain to get here, you know. My own mother's visited me once in all the years I've lived here. You really believe she wasn't coming to see someone specific?'

Lambiase shifts Maya in his lap. 'I've been thinking about that. Maybe she didn't have a plan of where she was going. Maybe she just took the first train and then the first bus and then the first boat and this is where she ended up.'

A.J. nods out of politeness, but he doesn't believe in random acts. He is a reader, and what he believes in is narrative construction. If a gun appears in act one, that gun had better go off by act three.

'Maybe she wanted to die somewhere with nice scenery,' Lambiase adds. 'So the lady from the Department of Children and Family Services (DCF) will be coming to get this little bundle of joy on Monday. Since the mother didn't have any family and the paternity is unknown, they'll have to find a foster home for her.'

A.J. counts the cash in the drawer. 'Kind of rough for kids in the system, no?'

'It can be,' Lambiase says. 'But this young, she'll probably do all right.'

A.J. recounts the cash in the drawer. 'You said the mother had been through the foster system?'

Lambiase nods.

'Suppose she thought the kid would stand a better chance in a bookstore.'

'Who can say?'

'I'm not a religious man, Chief Lambiase. I don't believe in fate. My wife. She believed in fate.'

At that moment, Maya wakes and holds out her arms to A.J. He closes the drawer of the cash register and takes her from Lambiase. Lambiase thinks he hears the little girl call A.J. 'Daddy'.

'Ugh, I keep telling her not to call me that,' A.J. says. 'But she won't listen.'

'Kids get ideas,' Lambiase says.

'You want a glass of something?'

'Sure. Why not?'

A.J. locks the front door of the store and heads up the stairs. He sets Maya on the futon and goes out to the main room of the house.

'I can't keep a baby,' A.J. says firmly. 'I haven't slept in two nights. She's a terrorist! She wakes up at, like, insane times. Three forty-five in the morning seems to be when her day begins. I live alone. I'm poor. You can't raise a baby on books alone.'

'True,' Lambiase says.

'I'm barely keeping myself together,' A.J. continues. 'She's worse than a puppy. And a man like me shouldn't even have a puppy. She's not potty-trained, and I have no idea how to do that kind of thing or any of the related matters either. Plus, I've never really liked babies. I like Maya, but . . . Conversation with her lacks, to say the least. We talk about Elmo, and I can't stand him, by the way, but other than that, it's mainly about her. She's totally self-centred.'

'Babies do tend to be that way,' Lambiase says. 'The conversation will probably improve when she knows more words.'

'And she always wants to read the same book. And it's, like, the crappiest board book. *The Monster at the End of This Book*?'

Lambiase says he hasn't heard of it.

'Well, believe you me. She's got terrible taste in books.' A.J. laughs.

Lambiase nods and drinks his wine. 'Nobody's saying you have to keep her.'

'Yeah, yeah, of course. But do you think I could have some sort of say in where she ended up? She's an awfully smart little thing. Like she already knows the alphabet and I even got her to understand alphabetical order. I'd hate to see her land with some jerks who didn't appreciate that. As I was saying before, I don't believe in fate. But I do feel a sense of responsibility toward her. That young woman did leave her in my care.'

'That young woman was out of her mind,' Lambiase says. 'She was an hour away from drowning herself.'

'Yeah.' A.J. frowns. 'You're right.' A cry from the other room. A.J. excuses himself. 'I should go check on her,' he says.

By the end of the weekend, Maya is in need of a bath. Though he would rather leave such an intimate activity to the state of Massachusetts, A.J. doesn't want to surrender her to social services looking like a miniature Miss Havisham. It takes A.J. several Google searches to determine bathing protocol: *appropriate temperature bath water two-year-old; can a two-year-old use grown-up shampoo?; how does a father go about cleaning a two-year-old girl's private parts without being a pervert?; how high to fill tub — toddler; how to prevent a two-year-old from accidentally drowning in tub; general rules for bath safety*, and so on.

He washes Maya's hair with hemp-based shampoo that used to belong to Nic. Long after he had donated or thrown away everything else of his wife's, he could not quite bring himself to discard her bath products.

A.J. rinses her hair, and Maya begins to sing.

'What is that you're singing?'

'Song,' she says.

'What song is that?'

'La la. Booya. La la.'

A.J. laughs. 'Yeah, that's gibberish to me, Maya.'

She splashes him.

'Mama?' she asks after a while.

'No, I'm not your mother,' A.J. says.

'Gone,' Maya says.

'Yes,' A.J. says. 'She probably isn't coming back.'

Maya thinks about this and then nods. 'You sing.'

'I'd rather not.'

'Sing,' she says.

The girl has lost her mother. He supposes it's the least he can do.

There is no time to Google appropriate songs for babies. Before he met his wife, A.J. had sung second tenor for the Footnotes, Princeton's all-male a cappella group. When A.J. fell for Nic, it was the Footnotes who had suffered, and after a semester of missed rehearsals he had been axed from the group. He thinks back to the last Footnotes show, which had been a tribute to eighties music. For his bathtub performance, he follows the programme pretty closely, beginning with '99 Luftballons' then segueing into 'Get out of My Dreams, Get into My Car'. For the finale, 'Love in an Elevator'. He only feels mildly foolish.

She claps when he is finished. 'Again,' she commands. 'Again.'

'That show runs one performance.' He lifts her out of the tub and then he towels her off, wiping between each perfect toe.

'Luftballon,' Maya says. 'Luft you.'

'What?'

'Love you,' she says.

'You're clearly responding to the power of a cappella.'

She nods. 'Love you.'

'Love me? You don't even know me,' A.J. says. 'Little girl, you shouldn't go throwing around your love so easily.' He pulls her to him. 'We've had a good run. This has been a delightful and, for me, at least, memorable seventy-two hours, but some people aren't meant to be in your life for ever.'

She looks at him with her big blue sceptical eyes. 'Love you,' she repeats.

A.J. towels her hair then gives her head an appraising sniff. 'I worry for you. If you love everyone, you'll end up having hurt feelings most of the time. I suppose, relative to the length of your life, you feel as if you've known me a rather long time. Your perspective of time is really very warped, Maya. But I am old and soon, you'll forget you even knew me.'

Molly Klock knocks on the door to the apartment. 'The woman from the state is downstairs. Is it okay for me to send her up?'

A.J. nods.

He pulls Maya into his lap, and they wait, listening as the social worker ascends the creaky stairs. 'Now don't be afraid, Maya. This lady's going to find a perfectly good home for you. Better than here. You can't spend the rest of your life sleeping on a futon, you know. The kind of people who spend their lives as permanent guests on a futon are not the kind of people you want to know.'

The social worker's name is Jenny. A.J. cannot recall ever having met an adult woman named Jenny. If Jenny were a book, she would be a paperback just out of the box – no dog ears, no waterlogging, no creases in her spine. A.J. would prefer a social worker with some obvious wear. He imagines the synopsis on the back of the Jenny story: *When plucky Jenny from Fairfield, Connecticut, took a job as a social worker in the big city, she had no idea what she was getting into . . .*

'Is it your first day?' A.J. asks.

'No,' Jenny says, 'I've been doing this a little while.' Jenny smiles at Maya. 'What a beauty you are.'

Maya buries her face in A.J.'s hoodie.

'You two seem very bonded.' Jenny makes a note in her pad. 'So it's like this. From here, I'll take Maya back to Boston. As her caseworker, I'll fill out some paperwork for her – she obviously can't do that herself, ha ha. She'll be assessed by a medical doctor and a psychologist.'

'She seems pretty healthy and well adjusted to me,' A.J. says.

'It's good that you've observed that. The doctors will be on the lookout for developmental delays, illnesses, and other things that might not be obvious to the untrained eye. After that, Maya will be placed with one of our many pre-approved foster families, and—'

A.J. interrupts. 'How does a foster family get pre-approved? Is it as easy as, say, getting a department store credit card?'

'Ha ha. No, of course, there are more steps to it than that. Applications, home visits—'

A.J. interrupts again. 'What I mean to say, Jenny, is how do you make sure you aren't placing an innocent child with a complete psychopath?'

'Well, Mr Fikry, we certainly don't start from the point of view that everyone who wants to foster a child is a psycho-path, but we do extensively vet all our foster families.'

'I worry because . . . well, Maya's very bright, but she's also very trusting,' A.J. says.

'Bright but trusting. Good insight. I'll write that down.' Jenny does. 'So after I place her in an emergency, *non-psychopathic*' – she smiles at A.J. – 'foster family, I go to work again. I try to see if anyone in her extended family wants to claim her and if that's a no, I start trying to find a per-manent situation for Maya.'

'You mean adoption.'

'Yes, exactly. Very good, Mr Fikry.' Jenny doesn't have to explain all this, but she likes to make Good Samaritans like A.J. feel like their time has been valued. 'By the way, I really have to thank you,' she says. 'We need more people like you who are willing to take an interest.' She holds out her arms to Maya. 'Ready, sweetie?'

A.J. pulls Maya closer to him. He takes a deep breath. Is he really going to do this? *Yes, I am. Dear God.* 'You say that Maya will be placed in a temporary foster home? Couldn't I just as well be that home?'

The social worker purses her lips. 'All our foster families have gone through an application process, Mr Fikry.'

'The thing is . . . I know it's not orthodox, but the mother left me this note.' He hands the note to Jenny. 'She wanted me to have this child, you see. It was her last wish. I think it's only right that I should keep her. I don't want her moved into some foster home when she has a perfectly good home right here. I Googled the matter last night.'

'Google,' says Maya.

'She's taken a fancy to that word, I don't know why.'

'What "matter"?' Jenny asks.

'I'm not obligated to turn her over when it's the mother's wish that I should have her,' A.J. explains.

'Daddy,' says Maya as if on cue.

Jenny looks from A.J.'s eyes to Maya's. Both sets are annoyingly determined. She sighs. She had thought the afternoon would be simple, but now it's starting to get complex.

Jenny sighs again. It is not her first day, though she only finished her master's in social work eighteen months ago. She is either bright-eyed or inexperienced enough to want to help them. Still, he's a single man, who lives above a store. *The paperwork is going to be ridiculous,* she thinks. 'Help me out here, Mr Fikry. Tell me you have a background in education or child development or some such.'

'Um ... I was on my way to a PhD in American Literature before I quit that to open this bookstore. My specialty was Edgar Allan Poe. "The Fall of the House of Usher" is a decent primer on what not to do with children.'

'That's something,' Jenny says, by which she means it's *something* entirely unhelpful. 'You're sure you're up to this? It's an enormous financial and emotional and time commitment.'

'No,' A.J. says, 'I'm not sure. But I think Maya has as good a chance with me as with anyone else. I can watch her while I work, and we like each other, I think.'

'Love you,' Maya says.

'Yes, she keeps saying that,' A.J. says. 'I warned her about giving love that hasn't yet been earned, but honestly, I think it's the influence of that insidious Elmo. He loves everyone, you know?'

'I'm familiar with Elmo,' Jenny says. She wants to cry. There is going to be so much paperwork. And that's just for the foster placement. The adoption proper's going to be murder, and Jenny will be the one who has to make the two-hour trip to Alice Island every time someone from DCF has to check on Maya and A.J. 'Okay, you two, I have to call my boss.' As a girl, Jenny Bernstein, product of two stable and loving parents from Medford, Massachusetts, had adored orphan stories like *Anne of Green Gables* and *A Little Princess*. She has recently begun to suspect that the sinister effect of repeated reading of these stories was what led her to choose social work as a profession. In general, the profession had turned out to be less romantic than her readings had led her to believe. Yesterday, one of her former classmates discovered a foster mother who had starved a sixteen-year-old teenage boy down to forty-two pounds. All the neighbours had thought the teen was a six-year-old child. 'I still want to believe in happy endings,' the classmate had said, 'but it's getting hard.' Jenny smiles at Maya. What a lucky little girl, she thinks.

That Christmas and for weeks after, Alice buzzes with the news that A.J. Fikry the widower/bookstore owner has taken in an abandoned child. It is the most gossip-worthy story Alice has had in some time – probably since *Tamerlane* was stolen – and what is of particular interest is the character of A.J. Fikry. The town had always considered him to be snobbish and cold, and it seems inconceivable that such a man would adopt a baby just because it was abandoned in his store. The town florist tells a story about leaving a pair of sunglasses in Island Books and coming back less than one day later to find that A.J. had thrown them out. 'He said his store had no room for a lost-and-found. And that's what happens to very nice, vintage Ray-Bans!' the florist says. 'Can you imagine what will happen to an actual human being?' Furthermore, for years, A.J. had been asked to participate in town life – to sponsor soccer teams, to patronize bake sales, to buy ads in the high school yearbook. The man had always declined, and not always politely either. They can only conclude that A.J. has grown soft since losing *Tamerlane*.

The mothers of Alice fear that the baby will be neglected. What can a single man know about child rearing? They make it their cause to stop by the store as often as possible to give A.J. advice and sometimes small gifts – old baby furniture, clothes, blankets, toys. The mothers are surprised to find Maya to be a sufficiently clean, happy and self-possessed little person. Only after they've left the store do they cluck about how tragic Maya's backstory is.

For his part, A.J. does not mind the visits. The advice he mainly ignores. The gifts he accepts (though he does liberally curate and disinfect them after the women have left). He knows about the post-visit clucking and decides not to let it annoy him. He leaves a jug of Purell on the counter next to a sign that commands PLEASE DISINFECT BEFORE HANDLING THE INFANTA. Besides, the women do actually know a few things that he doesn't know, things about potty training (bribery works) and teething (fancy ice-cube trays) and vaccinations (you can skip the chicken pox one). It turns out that, as a source of child-rearing advice, Google is wide but not, alas, terribly deep.

While visiting the baby, many of the women even buy books and magazines. A.J. begins to stock books because he thinks the women will enjoy discussing them. For a while, the circle responds to contemporary stories about overly capable women trapped in troubled marriages; they like if she has an affair – not that they themselves have (or will admit to having had) affairs. The fun is in judging these women. Women who abandon their children are a bridge too far, although husbands who have terrible accidents are usually received warmly (extra points if he dies, and she finds love again). Maeve Binchy is popular for a while, until

Margene, who in another life had been an investment banker, raises the complaint that Binchy's work is too formulaic. 'How many times can I read about a woman married too young to a bad, handsome man in a stifling Irish town?' A.J. is encouraged to expand his curatorial efforts. 'If we're going to have this book group,' Margene says, 'we may as well have some variety.'

'Is this a book group?' A.J. says.

'Isn't it?' Margene says. 'You didn't think all this child-rearing advice came for free, did you?'

In April, *The Paris Wife*. In June, *A Reliable Wife*. In August, *American Wife*. In September, *The Time Traveler's Wife*. In December, he runs out of decent books with *wife* in the title. They read *Bel Canto*.

'And it wouldn't hurt you to expand the picture-book section,' Penelope, who always looks exhausted, suggests. 'The kids should have something to read when they're here, too.' The women bring their own little ones for Maya to play with, so it only makes sense. Not to mention, A.J. is tired of reading *The Monster at the End of This Book*, and though he has never been particularly interested in picture books before, he decides to make himself an expert. He wants Maya to read *literary* picture books if such a thing exists. And preferably modern ones. And preferably, preferably feminist ones. Nothing with princesses. It turns out that these works most definitely do exist. One night, he finds himself saying, 'Formally, the picture book has a similar elegance to the short story. Do you know what I mean, Maya?'

She nods seriously and turns the page.

'The talent of some of these people is astounding,' A.J. says. 'I honestly had no idea.'

Maya taps on the book. They are reading *Little Pea*, the story of a pea who has to eat all his sweets before he can have vegetables for dessert.

'It's called irony, Maya,' A.J. says.

'Iron,' she says. She makes an ironing gesture.

'Irony,' he repeats.

Maya cocks her head, and A.J. decides that he will teach her about irony some other day.

Chief Lambiase is a frequent visitor to the store, and to justify these visits, he buys books. Because Lambiase doesn't believe in wasting money, he reads the books, too. At first, he had mainly bought mass-market paperbacks – Jeffery Deaver and James Patterson (or whoever writes for James Patterson) – and then A.J. graduates him to trade paperbacks by Jo Nesbø and Elmore Leonard. Both authors are hits with Lambiase, so A.J. promotes him again to Walter Mosley and then Cormac McCarthy. A.J.'s most recent recommendation is Kate Atkinson's *Case Histories*.

Lambiase wants to talk about the book as soon as he gets to the store. 'So the thing is, at first I kind of hated the book, but then it grew on me, yeah.' He leans on the counter. 'Because, you know, it's about a detective. But it moves kind of slow and most things go unsolved. But then I thought, That's how life is. That's how the job really is.'

'There's a sequel,' A.J. informs him.

Lambiase nods. 'Not sure I'm on board for that yet. Sometimes I like everything solved. Villains get punished.

Good guys triumph. That sort of thing. Maybe another one of those Elmore Leonards, though. Hey A.J., I've been thinking. Maybe you and me could start a book club for law enforcement officers? Like, other cops I know might like reading some of these stories, and I'm the chief, so I'd make them buy books here. It wouldn't have to only be cops. It could be law enforcement enthusiasts, too.' Lambiase squeezes Purell on his hands and bends down to pick up Maya.

'Hey, pretty girl. How you doing?'

'Adopted,' she says.

'That is a very big word.' Lambiase looks at A.J. 'Hey, is this square? Did this really happen?'

The process had taken the average amount of time, concluding the September before Maya's third birthday. The major strikes against A.J. had included his lack of a driver's licence (he had never gotten one on account of his seizures) and, of course, the fact that he is a single man who had never raised a child or even a dog or a houseplant. Ultimately, A.J.'s education, his strong ties to the community (i.e., the bookstore), and the fact that the mother had wanted Maya to be placed with him had outweighed the strikes.

'Congratulations to my favourite book people!' Lambiase says. He throws Maya in the air, then catches her and sets her on the ground. He leans across the counter to shake A.J.'s hand. 'Naw. I gotta hug you, man. This is hug-worthy news,' the cop says. Lambiase moves behind the counter to embrace A.J.

'Let's have a toast,' A.J. says.

A.J. hoists Maya to his hip, and the two men go upstairs. A.J. puts Maya to bed, which takes for ever (the intricate affairs of her toilet and two entire picture books), and Lambiase gets the bottle started.

'You gonna christen her now?' Lambiase asks.

'I'm neither Christian nor particularly religious,' A.J. says. 'So no.'

Lambiase considers this, drinks a bit more wine. 'You didn't ask for my two cents, but you ought to at least have a party to introduce her to people. She's Maya Fikry now, right?'

A.J. nods.

'People should know this. You gotta give her a middle name, too. Plus, I think I ought to be her godfather,' Lambiase says.

'What would that entail exactly?'

'Well, let's say the kid's twelve and she gets caught shoplifting at the pharmacy. I'd probably use my influence to intervene.'

'Maya would never do that.'

'That's what all parents think,' Lambiase says. 'Basically, I'd be your back-up, A.J. People should have back-ups.' Lambiase finishes off his glass. 'I'd help you with the party.'

'What would a not-christening party entail?' A.J. asks.

'It's not a big deal. You have it in the store. You buy Maya a new dress from Filene's Basement. I bet Ismay can help with that. You get food from Costco. Those big muffins, maybe? My sister says they've got a thousand calories a piece. And some frozen stuff. Nice stuff. Coconut shrimp. A big hunk of Stilton. And since it's not going to be Christian—'

A.J. interrupts. 'For the record, it's not going to be un-Christian either.'

'Right. My point is you can serve booze. And we invite your brother-in-law and sister-in-law and those ladies you hang out with and everyone else who has taken an interest in little Maya, which I'll tell you, A.J., is just about the whole town. And I'd say some nice words as the godfather, if you decide to go that way. Not a prayer, 'cause I know you're not into that. But you know I'd wish the little girl well on this journey we call life. And you'd thank everyone for coming. We all raise a glass to Maya. Everyone goes home happy.'

'So it's basically like a book party.'

'Yeah, sure.' Lambiase has never been to a book party.

'I hate book parties,' A.J. says.

'But you run the bookstore,' Lambiase says.

'It's a problem,' A.J. admits.

Maya's not-christening party is held the week before Halloween. Aside from several of the children in attendance wearing Halloween costumes, the party is indistinguishable from either a *christening* christening or a book party. A.J. watches Maya in her pink party dress, and he feels a vaguely familiar, slightly intolerable bubbling inside of him. He wants to laugh out loud or punch a wall. He feels drunk or at least carbonated. Insane. At first, he thinks this is happiness, but then he determines it's love. *Fucking love*, he thinks. *What a bother.* It's completely gotten in the way of his plan to drink himself to death, to drive his business to ruin. The most annoying thing about it is that once a person gives a shit about one thing, he finds he has to start giving a shit about everything.

No, the most annoying thing about it is that he's even started to like Elmo. There are Elmo paper plates on the folding table with the coconut shrimp and A.J. had blithely gone to multiple stores to find them. Across the room in Best Sellers, Lambiase is giving a speech that consists of clichés, albeit heartfelt and applicable ones: how A.J. has turned lemons into lemonade, how Maya is a silver-lined cloud, how God's closed door/open window policy really does apply here, and so forth. He smiles at A.J., and A.J. raises his glass and smiles back. And then, despite the fact that A.J. does not believe in God, he closes his eyes and thanks whomever, the higher power, with all his porcupine heart.

Ismay, who A.J. has made the godmother, grabs his hand. 'Sorry to abandon you, but I'm not feeling well,' she says.

'Was it Lambiase's speech?' A.J. says.

'I might be getting a cold. I'm going home.'

A.J. nods. 'Call me later, okay?'

It is Daniel who calls later. 'Ismay's in the hospital,' he says flatly. 'Another miscarriage.'

That makes two in the last year, five total. 'How is she?' A.J. asks.

'She's lost some blood and she's tired. She's a sturdy old mare, though.'

'She is.'

'It's a bad business, but unfortunately,' Daniel says, 'I've got to catch an early flight to Los Angeles. The movie people are buzzing.' The movie people are always buzzing in Daniel's stories, though none of them ever seem to sting. 'Would you mind going to check on her at the hospital, make sure she gets home all right?'

Lambiase drives A.J. and Maya to the hospital. A.J. leaves Maya in the waiting room with Lambiase and goes in to see Ismay.

Her eyes are red; her skin, pale. 'I'm sorry,' she says when she sees A.J.

'For what, Ismay?'

'I deserve this,' she says.

'You don't,' A.J. says. 'You shouldn't say that.'

'Daniel's an asshole for making you come out,' Ismay says.

'I was glad to,' A.J. says.

'He cheats on me. Do you know that? He cheats on me all the time.'

A.J. doesn't say anything, but he does know. Daniel's philandering is not a secret.

'Of course you know,' Ismay says in a husky voice. 'Everyone knows.'

A.J. says nothing.

'You do know, but you won't talk about it. Some misguided male code, I suppose.'

A.J. looks at her. Her shoulders are bony under the hospital gown, but her abdomen is still slightly round.

'I look a mess,' she says. 'That's what you're thinking.'

'No, I was noticing that you're growing out your hair. It's nice that way.'

'You're sweet,' she says. At that moment, Ismay sits up and tries to kiss A.J. on the mouth.

A.J. leans away from her. 'The doctor says you can go home right now if you'd like.'

'I thought my sister was an idiot when she married you, but now I see you're not that bad. The way you are with Maya. The way you are now, showing up. Showing up is what counts, A.J.

'I think I'd rather stay here tonight,' she says, flipping away from A.J. 'There's no one at my house, and I don't want to be that alone. What I said before is true. Nic was the good girl. I'm bad. I married a bad man, too. And I know that bad people deserve what they get, but oh, how we hate to be alone.'

What Feels Like the World

1985/Richard Bausch

Chubby girl lives with grandfather; trains for elementary school gymnastics exhibition.

You will be amazed by how much you care whether that little girl makes it over the vault. Bausch is able to wring exquisite tension from such a seemingly slight episode (though obviously this is the point), and this should be your takeaway: a vaulting exhibition can have every bit as much drama as a plane crash.

I did not encounter this story until after I became a father so I cannot say if I would have liked it as well P.M. (pre-Maya). I have gone through phases in my life when I am more in the mood for short stories. One of those phases coincided with your toddlerhood – what time had I for novels, my girl?

– A.J.F.

Maya usually wakes before the sun comes up, when the only sound is A.J. snoring in the other room. In footed pyjamas, she pads across the main room to A.J.'s bedroom. At first, she whispers, 'Daddy, Daddy.' If that doesn't work, she says his name and if that still doesn't work, she yells it. And if words are not enough, she jumps on the bed, though she would rather not resort to such shenanigans. Today he wakes when she has only reached talking level. 'Awake,' she says. 'Downstairs.'

The place Maya loves most is downstairs because downstairs is the store, and the store is the best place in the world.

'Pants,' A.J. mumbles. 'Coffee.' His breath smells like socks wet from snow.

There are sixteen stairs until you get to the bookstore. Maya slides her bottom down each one because her legs are too short to manage the flight with confidence. She toddles across the store, past the books that don't have pictures in them, past the greeting cards. She runs her hand across the magazines, gives the rotating stand with the bookmarks a spin. Good morning, magazines! Good morning, bookmarks! Good morning, books! Good morning, store!

The walls of the bookstore have wood panels up to just above her head, but beyond that is blue wallpaper. Maya can't reach the paper unless she has a chair. The wallpaper has a bumpy, swirling pattern, and it is pleasing to rub her face against it. She will read the word 'damask' in a book one day and think, *Yes, of course that's what it's called.* In contrast, the word *wainscoting* will come as a huge disappointment.

The store is fifteen Mayas wide and twenty Mayas long. She knows this because she once spent an afternoon measuring it by laying her body across the room. It is fortunate that it is not more than thirty Mayas long because that is as far as she could count on the day the measurements were taken.

From her vantage point on the floor, people are shoes. In the summer, sandals. In the winter, boots. Molly Klock sometimes wears red superhero boots up to her knees. A.J. is black sneakers with white toes. Lambiase wears finger-crushing Bigfoot shoes. Ismay wears flats that look like insects or jewels. Daniel Parish wears brown loafers with a penny in them.

Just before the store opens at 10 a.m., she goes to her station, which is the row with all the picture books.

The first way Maya approaches a book is to smell it. She strips the book of its jacket, then holds it up to her face and wraps the boards around her ears. Books typically smell like Daddy's soap, grass, the sea, the kitchen table and cheese.

She studies the pictures and tries to tease a story out of them. It is tiring work, but even at three years old, she recognizes some of the tropes. For instance, animals are not always animals in picture books. They sometimes represent parents and children. A bear wearing a tie might be a father. A bear with a blond wig might be a mother. You can tell a lot about a story from the pictures, but the pictures sometimes give you the wrong idea. She would prefer to know the words.

Assuming no interruptions, she can make it through seven books in a morning. However, there are always interruptions. Maya mainly likes customers, though, and tries to be polite to them. She understands the business she and A.J. are in. When children come into her row, she always makes sure to stick a book into their hands. The children wander up to the cash register, and more often than not the accompanying guardian will buy what the child is holding. 'Oh my, did you pick that yourself?' the parent will ask.

Once, someone had asked A.J. if Maya was his. 'You're both black but not the same kind of black.' Maya remembers this because the remark had made A.J. use a tone of voice she had never heard him use with a customer.

'What is *the same kind of black*?' A.J. had asked.

'No, I didn't mean to offend you,' the person had said and then the flip-flops had backed their way to the door, leaving without making a purchase.

What *is* 'the same kind of black'? She looks at her hands and wonders.

Here are some other things she wonders about.

How do you learn to read?

Why do grown-ups like books without pictures?

Will Daddy ever die?

What is for lunch?

Lunch is around one and comes from the sandwich shop. She has grilled cheese. A.J. has a turkey club. She likes to go to the sandwich shop, but she always holds A.J.'s hand. She would not want to be left in a sandwich shop.

In the afternoon, she draws reviews. An apple means the book's smell is approved. A block of cheese means the book is ripe. A self-portrait means she likes the pictures. She signs these reports MAYA and passes them on to A.J. for his approval.

She likes to write her name.

MAYA.

She knows her last name is Fikry, but she doesn't know how to write that yet.

Sometimes, after the customers and the employees have left, she thinks that she and A.J. are the only people in the world. No one else seems as real as he does. Other people are shoes for different seasons, nothing more. A.J. can touch the wallpaper without getting on a chair, can operate the cash register while talking on the phone, can lift heavy boxes of books over his head, uses impossibly long words, knows everything about everything. Who could compare to A.J. Fikry?

She does not think of her mother almost ever.

She knows that her mother is dead. And she knows that dead is when you go to sleep and you do not wake up. She feels very sorry for her mother because people who don't wake up can't go downstairs to the bookstore in the morning.

Maya knows that her mother left her in Island Books. But maybe that's what happens to all children at a certain age. Some children are left in shoe stores. And some children are left in toy stores. And some children are left in sandwich shops. And your whole life is determined by what store you get left in. She does not want to live in the sandwich shop.

Later, when she is older, she will think about her mother more.

In the evening, A.J. changes his shoes, then puts her in a stroller. It is getting to be a tight fit, but she likes the ride so she tries not to complain. She likes hearing A.J. breathing. And she likes seeing the world moving by so fast. And sometimes, he sings. And sometimes he tells her stories. He tells her how he had a book called *Tamerlane* once and it was worth as much as all the books in the store combined.

Tamerlane, she says, liking the mystery and the music of the syllables.

'And that is how you got your middle name.'

At night, A.J. tucks her in bed. She does not like to go to bed even if she is tired. The offer of a story is the best way for A.J. to persuade her to sleep. 'Which one?' he says.

He's been nagging her to stop choosing *The Monster at the End of This Book*, so she pleases him by saying, '*Caps for Sale*'.

She has heard the story before, but she can't make sense of it. It is about a man who sells colourful hats. He takes a nap, and his hats get stolen by monkeys. She hopes this will never happen to A.J.

Maya is furrowing her brow, clutching A.J.'s arm.

'What is it?' A.J. asks.

Why do monkeys want hats? Maya wonders. Monkeys are animals. Maybe the monkeys, like the bear in the wig who is a mother, represent something else, but what . . . ? She has thoughts but not words.

'Read,' she says.

Sometimes A.J. has a woman come to the store to read books aloud to Maya and the other children. The woman gesticulates and mugs, raising and lowering her voice for dramatic effect. Maya wants to tell her to relax. She is used to the way A.J. reads – soft and low. She is used to him.

A.J. reads, '. . . on the very top, a bunch of red caps.'

The picture shows a man in many coloured caps.

Maya puts her hand over A.J.'s to stop him from turning the page just yet. She scans her eyes from the picture to the page and back again. All at once, she knows that r-e-d is red, knows it like she knows her name is Maya, like she knows A.J. Fikry is her father, like she knows the best place in the world is Island Books.

'What is it?' he asks.

'Red,' she says. She takes his hand and moves it so it is pointing to the word.

A Good Man Is Hard to Find

1953/Flannery O'Connor

Family trip goes awry. It's Amy's favourite. (She seems so sweet on the surface, no?) Amy and I do not always have the exact same taste in things, but this I like.

When she told me it was her favourite, it suggested to me strange and wonderful things about her character that I had not guessed, dark places that I might like to visit.

People tell boring lies about politics, God and love. You know every-thing you need to know about a person from the answer to the question: What is your favourite book?

— A.J.F.

The second week of August, just before Maya starts kindergarten, she gets a matching set of glasses (round, red frames) and chickenpox (round, red bumps). A.J. curses the mother who had told him that the chickenpox vaccine was optional as the chickenpox is indeed a pox on their house. Maya is miserable, and A.J. is miserable because Maya is miserable. The marks plague her face, and the air conditioner breaks, and no one in their house can sleep. A.J. brings her icy washcloths, removes skin from tangerine slices, puts socks on her hands and stands guard at her bedside.

Day three, four in the morning, Maya falls asleep. A.J. is exhausted but restless. He had asked one of the clerks to grab a couple of galleys from the basement for him. Unfortunately, the clerk is new, and she had picked books from the TO BE RECYCLED pile, not the TO BE READ pile. A.J. doesn't want to leave Maya's side so he decides to read one of the old, rejected galleys. The top one in the pile is a young-adult fantasy novel in which the main character is dead. *Ugh*, A.J. thinks. Two of his least favourite things (post-mortem narrators and young-adult novels) in one book. He tosses the paper carcass aside. The second one in the pile is a memoir written by an eighty-year-old man, a lifelong bachelor and onetime science writer for various Midwestern newspapers, who married at the age of seventy-eight. His bride died two years after the wedding at the age of eighty-three. *The Late Bloomer* by Leon Friedman. The book is familiar to A.J., but he's not sure why. He opens the galley and a business card falls out: AMELIA LOMAN, KNIGHTLEY PRESS. Yes, he remembers now.

Of course, he has encountered Amelia Loman in the years since that awkward first meeting. They have had a handful of cordial e-mails, and she comes triannually to report on Knightley's hottest prospects. After spending ten or so afternoons with her, he's recently come to the conclusion that she is good at her job. She is informed about her list and greater literary trends. She is upbeat but not an overseller. She is sweet with Maya, too – usually remembers to bring the girl a book from one of Knightley's children's lines. Above all, Amelia Loman is professional, which means she has never brought up A.J.'s poor conduct the day they met. God, he'd been awful to her. As penance, he decides to give *The Late Bloomer* a chance, though it is still not his type of thing.

'I am eighty-one years old, and statistically speaking, I should have died 4.7 years ago,' the book begins.

At five a.m., A.J. closes the book and gives it a pat.

Maya wakes, feeling better. 'Why are you crying?'

'I was reading,' A.J. says.

She doesn't recognize the number, but Amelia Loman picks up on the first ring.

'Amelia, hello. This is A. J. Fikry from Island. I wasn't expecting you to answer.'

'It's true,' she says, laughing. 'I'm the last person left in the entire world who still answers her phone.'

'Yes,' he says, 'you might be.'

'The Catholic Church is thinking of making me a saint.'

'Saint Amelia who answered the phone,' A.J. says.

'Are we still on for two weeks from now, or do you have to cancel?' Amelia asks. He has never called her before, and she assumes this must be the reason.

'Oh no, nothing like that. I was just planning to leave you a message, actually.'

Amelia speaks in monotone. 'Hi, you've reached the voicemail of Amelia Loman. Beep.'

'Um.'

'Beep,' Amelia repeats. 'Go ahead. Leave your message.'

'Um, hi, Amelia. This is A. J. Fikry. I've just finished reading a book you recommended to me—'

'Oh yeah, which one?'

'That's odd. Voicemail seems to be talking back to me. It's one from several years back. *The Late Bloomer* by Leon Friedman.'

'Don't go breaking my heart, A.J. That was my absolute favourite from four winter lists ago. No one wanted to read it. I loved that book. I still love that book! I'm the queen of lost causes, though.'

'Maybe it was the jacket,' A.J. says lamely.

'Lamentable jacket. Old people's feet, flowers,' Amelia agrees. 'Like anyone wants to think about wrinkly old feet let alone buy a book with them on it. Paperback re-jacket didn't help anything either – black and white, more flowers. But jackets are the redheaded stepchildren of book publishing. We blame them for everything.'

'I don't know if you remember, but you gave *The Late Bloomer* to me the first time we met,' A.J. says.

Amelia pauses. 'Did I? Yes, that makes sense. That would have been around the time I started at Knightley.'

'Well, you know, literary memoirs aren't usually my thing, but this was spectacular in its small way. Wise and ...' He feels naked when speaking about things he loves.

'Go on.'

'Every word the right one and exactly where it should be. That's basically the highest compliment I can give. I'm only sorry it took me so long to read it.'

'Story of my life. What made you finally pick it up?'

'My little girl was sick, so—'

'Oh, poor Maya! I hope nothing serious!'

'Chickenpox. I was up all night with her, and it was the book nearest to me at the time.'

'I'm glad you finally read it,' Amelia says. 'I begged everyone I knew to read this book, and no one would listen except my mother and even she wasn't an easy sell.'

'Sometimes books don't find us until the right time.'

'Not much consolation for Mr Friedman,' Amelia adds.

'Well, I'm going to order a carton of the equally lamentably jacketed paperback. And in the summer, when the tourists are here, maybe we could have Mr Friedman in for an event.'

'If he lives that long,' Amelia says.

'Is he sick?' A.J. asks.

'No, but he's, like, ninety!'

A.J. laughs. 'Well, Amelia, I'll see you in two weeks, I guess.'

'Maybe next time you'll listen to me when I tell you something's the "best book of the winter list"!' Amelia says.

'Probably not. I'm old, set in my ways, contrary.'

'You're not that old,' she says.

'Not compared to Mr Friedman, I suppose.' A.J. clears his throat. 'When you're in town, maybe we could have dinner or something.'

It isn't at all uncommon for sales reps and booksellers to break bread, but Amelia detects a certain tone in A.J.'s voice. She clarifies. 'We can go over the new winter list.'

'Yes, of course,' A.J. answers too quickly. 'It's such a long trip for you to Alice. You'll be hungry. It's rude that I've never suggested it before.'

'Let's make it a late lunch, then,' Amelia says. 'I need to catch the last ferry back to Hyannis.'

A.J. decides to take Amelia to Pequod's, which is the second-nicest seafood restaurant on Alice Island. El Corazon, the nicest restaurant, is not open for lunch, and even if it had been, El Corazon would have seemed too romantic for what is only a business meeting.

A.J. arrives first, which gives him time to regret his choice. He has not been to Pequod's since before he adopted Maya, and its decor strikes him as embarrassing and touristy. The tasteful white table linens do not much distract from the harpoons, nets, and raincoats hanging from the walls, or the captain, carved out of a log, who welcomes you with a bucket of complimentary saltwater taffy. A fibreglass whale with tiny, sad eyes is mounted from the ceiling. A.J. senses the whale's judgment: *Should have gone with El Corazon, matey.*

Amelia is five minutes late. 'Pequod, like *Moby Dick*,' she says. She is wearing a dress made out of what looks like a re-purposed crocheted tablecloth over a vintage pink slip. She has a fake daisy in her curly blond hair and is wearing galoshes despite the fact that the day is sunny. A.J. thinks the galoshes make her seem like a Boy Scout, in a state of readiness and prepared for disaster.

'Do you like *Moby Dick*?' he asks.

'I hate it,' she says. 'And I don't say that about many things. Teachers assign it, and parents are happy because their kids are reading something of "quality". But it's forcing kids to read books like that that make them think they hate reading.'

'I'm surprised you didn't cancel when you saw the name of the restaurant.'

'Oh, I thought about it,' she says with mirth in her voice. 'But then I reminded myself that it's just a restaurant name and it probably won't affect the quality of the food too, too much. Plus I looked up the reviews online, and it sounded delicious.'

'You didn't trust me?'

'I like to think about what I'm going to eat before I get there. I like to' – she stretches out the word – 'an-ti-ci-pate.' She opens the menu. 'I see they've got several cocktails named after *Moby Dick* characters.' She turns the page. 'Anyway, if I hadn't wanted to eat here, I probably would have invented an allergy to shellfish.'

'Fictional food allergy. That's very devious of you,' A.J. says.

'Now I won't be able to use that trick with you.'

The waiter is dressed in a puffy white shirt that is clearly in conflict with his black glasses and spiky hair. The look is pirate hipster. 'Ahoy, landlubbers,' the waiter says flatly. 'Try a themed cocktail?'

'My standard drink is the old-fashioned, but how can a person be expected to resist a themed cocktail?' she says. 'One Queequeg, please.' She grabs the waiter's hand. 'Wait. Is it good?'

'Um,' the waiter says. 'The tourists seem to like them.'

'Well, if the tourists like them,' she says.

'Um, so I'm clear, does that mean you do or you don't want the cocktail?'

'I definitely want it,' Amelia says. 'Come what may.' She smiles at the waiter. 'I won't blame you if it's terrible.'

A.J. orders a glass of the house red.

'That's sad,' Amelia says. 'I bet you've gone your whole life without having a Queequeg despite the fact that you live here and you sell books and you probably even like *Moby Dick.*'

'You're obviously a more evolved person than I am,' A.J. says.

'Yes, I can see that. And after I have this cocktail, my whole life's probably going to change.'

The drinks arrive. 'Oh, look,' Amelia says. 'A shrimp with a little harpoon through it. That is an unexpected delight.' She takes out her phone and snaps a picture. 'I like to take pictures of my drinks.'

'They're like family,' A.J. says.

'They're *better* than family.' She raises her glass and clinks it to A.J.'s.

'How is it?' he asks.

'Salty, fruity, fishy. It's kind of like if a shrimp cocktail decided to make love to a Bloody Mary.'

'I like how you say, *make* love. The drink sounds disgusting, by the way.'

She takes another sip and shrugs. 'It's growing on me.'

'In what restaurant based on a novel would you have preferred to dine?' A.J. asks her.

'Oh, that's tough. This won't make any sense, but when I was in college I used to get really hungry when I was reading *The Gulag Archipelago*. All that description of Soviet prison bread and soup,' Amelia says.

'You're weird,' A.J. says.

'Thank you. Where would you go?' Amelia asks.

'This wouldn't be a restaurant per se, but I always wanted to try the Turkish Delight in Narnia. When I read *The Lion, the Witch and the Wardrobe* as a boy, I used to think that Turkish Delight must be incredibly delicious if it made Edmund betray his family,' A.J. says. 'I guess I must have told my wife this, because one year Nic gets a box for me for the holidays. And it turned out to be this powdery, gummy candy. I don't think I've ever been so disappointed in my entire life.'

'Your childhood was officially over right then.'

'I was never the same,' A.J. says.

'Maybe the White Witch's was different. Like, magical Turkish Delight tastes better.'

'Or maybe Lewis's point is that Edmund didn't need much coaxing to betray his family.'

'That's very cynical,' Amelia says.

'Have you *had* Turkish Delight, Amelia?'

'No,' she says.

'I'll have to get you some,' he says.

'What if I love it?' she asks.

'I'll probably think less of you.'

'Well, I won't lie just to get you to like me, A.J. One of my best qualities is my honesty.'

'You told me you would have faked a seafood allergy to get out of eating here,' A.J. says.

'Yes, but that was only so I wouldn't hurt an account's feelings. I'd never lie about something important like Turkish Delight.'

They order food and then Amelia takes out the winter catalogue from her tote bag. 'So, Knightley,' she says.

'Knightley,' he repeats.

She breezes through the winter list, ruthlessly flipping past the books he won't go for, emphasizing the publisher's great hopes, and saving her fanciest adjectives for her favourites. With some accounts, you mention if the book has blurbs, those often hyperbolic endorsements from established writers that appear on the back cover. A.J. is not one of those accounts. At their second or third meeting, he had referred to blurbs as 'the blood diamonds of publishing'. She knows him a little better now, and needless to say, this process is less painful for it. He trusts me more, she thinks, or maybe it's just that fatherhood has mellowed him. (It is wise to keep thoughts like this to yourself.) A.J. promises to read several of the ARCs.

'In less than four years, I hope,' Amelia says.

'I'll do my best to have them read in three.' He pauses.

'Let's order dessert,' he says. 'There must be a "whale of a sundae" or something.'

Amelia groans. 'That is truly an awful wordplay.'

'So if you don't mind my asking, why was *The Late Bloomer* your favourite book from that list? You're a young—'

'I'm not that young. I'm thirty-five.'

'That's still young,' A.J. says. 'What I mean is you probably haven't experienced much of what Mr Friedman describes. I look at you, and having read the book, I wonder what made you respond to it.'

'My, Mr Fikry, that's a very personal question.' She sips at the last of her second Queequeg. 'The main reason I loved the book was the quality of the writing, of course.'

'Of course. But that isn't enough.'

'Let's just say I'd been on many, many bad dates by the time *The Late Bloomer* came across my desk. I'm a romantic person, but sometimes these don't seem like romantic times to me. *The Late Bloomer* is a book about the possibility of finding great love at any age. Sounds clichéd, I know.'

A.J. nods.

'And you? Why did you like it?' Amelia asks.

'Quality of the prose, blah blah blah.'

'I thought we weren't allowed to say that!' Amelia says.

'You don't want to hear my sad stories, do you?'

'Sure I do,' she says. 'I love sad stories.'

He gives her the Cliffs Notes version of Nic's death. 'Friedman gets at something specific about what it is to lose someone. How it isn't one thing. He writes about how you lose and lose and lose.'

'When did she die?' Amelia asks.

'A while ago now. I was only a little older than you at the time.'

'That must have been a *long* while ago,' she says.

He ignores the barb. '*The Late Bloomer* really should have been a popular book.'

'I know. I'm thinking of having someone read a passage from it at my wedding.'

A.J. pauses. 'You're getting married, Amelia. Congratulations. Who's the lucky fellow?'

She stirs the harpoon around the tomato juice-tinted waters of her Queequeg, trying to recapture a shrimp that's gone AWOL. 'His name is Brett Brewer. I'd about given up when I met him online.'

A.J. drinks the bitter dregs of his second glass of wine. 'Tell me more.'

'He's in the military, serving overseas in Afghanistan.'

'Well done. You're marrying an American hero,' A.J. says.

'I guess I am.'

'I hate those guys,' he says. 'They make me feel totally inadequate. Tell me something shitty about him so that I feel better.'

'Well, he's not home much.'

'You must miss him.'

'I do. I get a lot of reading done, though.'

'That's good. Does he read, too?'

'No, actually. He's not much of a reader. But that's kind of interesting, right? I mean, it's interesting to be with someone whose, um, interests are so different than mine. I don't know why I keep saying "interests". The point is, he's a good man.'

'He's good to you?'

She nods.

'That's what counts. Anyway, nobody's perfect,' A.J. says. 'Someone probably made him read *Moby Dick* in high school.'

Amelia stabs her shrimp. 'Caught it,' she says. 'Your wife . . . was she a reader?'

'And a writer. I wouldn't worry about it, though. Reading's overrated. Look at all the good stuff on television. Stuff like *True Blood*.'

'Now you're making fun of me.'

'Bah! Books are for nerds,' A.J. says.

'Nerds like us.'

When the check comes, A.J. pays despite the fact that it is customary for the sales rep to pay in such situations. 'Are you sure?' Amelia asks.

A.J. tells her that she can pay next time.

Outside the restaurant, Amelia and A.J. shake hands, and the usual professional pleasantries are exchanged. She turns to walk back to the ferry, and one important second later he turns to walk to the bookstore.

'Hey A.J.,' she calls. 'There's something kind of heroic about being a bookseller, and there's also something kind of heroic about adopting a child.'

'I do what I can.' He bows. Halfway through the bow, he realizes that he is not the type of man who can pull off bowing and quickly rights himself. 'Thank you, Amelia.'

'My friends call me Amy,' she says.

*

Maya has never seen A.J. so occupied. 'Daddy,' she asks, 'why do you have so much homework?'

'Some of it's extracurricular,' he says.

'What's "extracurricular"?'

'I'd look it up if I were you.'

Reading an entire season's list, even the list of a modestly sized house like Knightley, is a major time commitment for a person with a chatty kindergartner and a small business. After he finishes each Knightley title, he sends Amelia an e-mail to tell her his thoughts. In his e-mails, he cannot bring himself to use the nickname 'Amy', though permission has been granted. Sometimes, if he really responds to something, he calls her. If he hates a book, he'll send a text: *Not for me*. For her part, Amelia has never received this much attention from an account.

Don't you have any other publishers to read? Amelia texts him.

A.J. thinks a long time about his reply. *None with sales reps I like as well as you* is his first draft, but he decides this is too presumptuous for a girl with an American hero fiancé. He redrafts *It's a compelling list for Knightley, I guess.*

A.J. orders so many Knightley titles that even Amelia's boss notices. 'I've never seen a little account like Island take so many of our books,' the boss says. 'New owner?'

'Same guy,' Amelia says. 'But he's different from when I first met him.'

'Well, you must have really done a number on him. That guy doesn't take what he can't sell,' the boss says. 'Harvey never came close to these kinds of orders with Island.'

Finally, A.J. gets to the last title. It's a charming memoir about motherhood, scrapbooking, and the writing life, written by a Canadian poet that A.J. has always liked. The book is only 150 pages, but it takes A.J. two weeks to get through it. He can't seem to read a chapter without falling asleep or being distracted by Maya. When he finishes it, he finds himself unable to craft a response. The writing is elegant enough, and he thinks the women who frequent his store could respond to it. The problem, of course, is that once he replies to Amelia, he'll be done with the Knightley winter catalogue, and he'll have no reason to contact Amelia until the summer list hits. He likes her, and he thinks it's possible that she might like him, despite that horrendous first meeting. But ... A. J. Fikry is not the kind of man who thinks it's okay to try to steal another man's fiancée. He doesn't believe in 'the one'. There are zillions of people in the world; no one is *that special*. Besides which, he barely knows Amelia Loman. What if, say, he did manage to steal her and it turned out they weren't compatible in bed?

Amelia texts him, *What's happening? Didn't you like?*

Not for me, unfortunately, A.J. replies. *Looking forward to seeing what's on Knightley's summer list. Yours, A.J.*

The response strikes Amelia as overly businesslike, dismissive. She thinks about picking up the phone but doesn't. She texts back, *While you're waiting, you should definitely watch TRUE BLOOD. True Blood* is Amelia's favourite television show. It has gotten to be a kind of joke with them that A.J. would like vampires if only he would watch *True Blood.* Amelia fancies herself a Sookie Stackhouse type.

Not gonna happen, Amy, A.J. writes. *See you in March.*

March is four and a half months away. By then, A.J. feels

sure, his little crush will have gone away or at least resolved itself into a more tolerable dormancy.

March is four and a half months away.

Maya asks him what's wrong, and he tells her that he's sad because he's not going to see his friend for a while.

'Amelia?' Maya asks.

'How do you know about her?'

Maya rolls her eyes, and A.J. wonders when and where she learned that gesture.

Lambiase hosts his Chief's Choice Book Club at the store that night (selection: *L.A. Confidential*), and after that, as is their tradition, he and A.J. share a bottle.

'I think I've met someone,' A.J. says after a glass has mellowed him.

'Good news,' Lambiase says.

'The problem is, she's affianced to someone else.'

'Bad timing,' Lambiase proclaims. 'I've been a police officer for twenty years now and I'll tell you, pretty much every bad thing in life is a result of bad timing, and every good thing is the result of good timing.'

'That seems terribly reductive.'

'Think about it. If *Tamerlane* hadn't gotten stolen, you wouldn't have left the door unlocked, and Marian Wallace wouldn't have left the baby in the store. Good timing is what that was.'

'True. But I met Amelia four years ago,' A.J. argues. 'I just didn't bother to notice her until a couple of months ago.'

'Still bad timing. Your wife had died. And then you had Maya.'

'It's not much consolation,' A.J. says.

'But hey, it's good to know your heart still works, right? Want me to set you up with someone?'

A.J. shakes his head.

'Come on,' Lambiase insists. 'I know everyone in town.'

'Unfortunately, it's a very small town.'

As a warm-up, Lambiase sets up A.J. with his cousin. The cousin has blond hair with black roots, overly plucked eyebrows, a heart-shaped face, and a high-pitched voice like Michael Jackson. She wears a low-cut top and a push-up bra, which creates a small, sad shelf for her name necklace to rest. Her name is Maria. In the middle of mozzarella sticks, they run out of conversation.

'What's your favourite book?' A.J. attempts to draw her out.

She chews on her mozzarella stick and clutches her Maria necklace like it's a rosary. 'This is some kind of a test, right?'

'No, there's no wrong answer,' A.J. says. 'I'm curious.'

She drinks her wine.

'Or you could say the book that had the greatest influence on your life. I'm trying to get to know you a little.'

She takes another sip.

'Or how about the last thing you read?'

'The last thing I read ...' She furrows her brow. 'The last thing I read was this menu.'

'And the last thing I read was your necklace,' he says. 'Maria.'

The meal is perfectly cordial after that. He never will find out what Maria reads.

Next, Margene from the store sets him up with her neighbour, a lively female firefighter named Rosie. Rosie has spiky black hair with a blue streak, exceptional arm muscles, a great big laugh and short nails she paints red with little orange flames. Rosie is a former college hurdles champion, and she likes to read sports history and particularly athletes' memoirs.

On their third date, she's in the middle of describing a dramatic section from José Canseco's *Juiced* when A.J. interrupts her, 'You know they're all ghostwritten?'

Rosie says she knows and she doesn't care. 'These high-performance individuals have been busy training and practising. When did they have time to learn to write books?'

'But these books ... My point is, they're essentially lies.'

Rosie cocks her head toward A.J. and taps her flame nails on the table. 'You're a snob, you know that? Makes you miss out on a lot.'

'I've been told that before.'

'All of life's in a sports memoir,' she says. 'You practise hard and you succeed, but eventually your body gives out and it's over.'

'Sounds like a latter-period Philip Roth novel,' he says.

Rosie crosses her arm. 'That's one of those things you say to sound smart, right?' she says. 'But, really, you're trying to make someone else feel stupid.'

That night in bed, after sex that feels more like wrestling, Rosie rolls away from him and says, 'I'm not sure I want to see you again.'

'I'm sorry if I hurt your feelings before,' he says as he puts his pants back on. 'The memoirs thing.'

She waves her hand. 'Don't worry about it. You can't help the way you are.'

He suspects she is right. He is a snob, not suited for relationships. He will raise his daughter, run his store, read his books, and that, he decides, will be more than enough.

At Ismay's insistence, it is determined that Maya should take dance. 'You don't want her to be deprived, do you?' Ismay says.

'Of course not,' A.J. says.

'Well,' Ismay says, 'dance is important, not just physically but socially too. You don't want her to end up stunted.'

'I don't know. The idea of enrolling a little girl in dance. Isn't that kind of an old-fashioned and sexist notion?'

A.J. is unsure whether Maya will be suited to dance. Even at six, she is cerebral – always with a book and content at home or at the store. 'She's not stunted,' he says. 'She reads chapter books now.'

'Not intellectually, obviously,' Ismay insists. 'But she seems to prefer your company to anyone else's, certainly anyone her own age, and that probably isn't healthy.'

'Why isn't it healthy?' Now A.J.'s spine is tingling unpleasantly.

'She's going to end up just like you,' Ismay says.

'And what would be wrong with that?'

Ismay gives him a look as if the answer should be obvious. 'Look, A.J., you two are your own little world. You never date—'

'I do date.'

'You never travel—'

A.J. interrupts. 'We aren't talking about me.'

'Stop being so argumentative. You asked me to be god-mother, and I'm telling you to enrol your daughter in dance. I'll pay for it, so don't you fight me any more.'

There is one dance studio on Alice Island and one class for girls aged five and six. The owner/teacher is Madame Olenska. She is in her sixties and though she is not over-weight, her skin hangs, suggesting that her bones have shrunken over the years. Her always bejewelled fingers seem to have one joint too many. The children are both fas-cinated and frightened by her. A.J. feels the same way. The first time he drops off Maya, Madame Olenska says, 'Mr Fikry, you are first man to set foot in this dance studio in twenty years. We must take advantage of you.'

In her Russian accent, this seems like a sexual invitation of some kind, but mainly what she requires is manual labour. For the holiday recital, he paints and constructs a large wooden crate to look like a child's block, hot-glue-guns googly eyes, bells and flowers, and fashions sparkly pipe cleaners into whiskers and antennae. (He suspects he will never get the glitter out from under his nails.)

He spends much of his free time that winter with Madame Olenska, and he learns a lot about her. For instance, Madame Olenska's star pupil is her daughter, who dances in a Broadway show and whom Madame Olenska hasn't spoken to in a decade. She wags her triple-jointed finger at him. 'Don't let that happen to you.' She looks dra-matically out of the window, then slowly turns back to A.J.

'You will buy ad in programme for bookstore, yes.' It is not a question. Island Books becomes the sole sponsor of *The Nutcracker, Rudolph and Friends*, and a holiday coupon for the store appears on the back page of the programme. A.J. goes even further, providing a gift basket of dance-themed books to be raffled off, with proceeds going to the Boston Ballet.

From the raffle table A.J. watches the show, exhausted and slightly fluish. As the acts are arranged according to skill, Maya's group is on first. She is an enthusiastic if not overly graceful mouse. She scurries with abandon. She wrinkles her nose in a recognizably mousy way. She wags her pipe-cleaner tail, which had been painstakingly coiled by him. He knows a career in dance is not in her future.

Ismay, who mans the table with him, hands him a Kleenex.

'Cold,' he says.

'Sure it is,' Ismay says.

At the end of the night, Madame Olenska says, 'Thank you, Mr Fikry. You are good man.'

'Maybe I've got a good kid.' He still needs to claim his mouse from the dressing room.

'Yes,' she says. 'But this is not enough. You must find yourself good woman.'

'I like my life,' A.J. says.

'You think child is enough, but child grows old. You think work is enough, but work is not warm body.' He suspects Madame Olenska has already tossed back a few Stolis.

'Happy holidays, Madame Olenska.'

Walking home with Maya, he is contemplating the

teacher's words. He has been alone for nearly six years. Grief is hard to bear, but alone, he has never much minded. Besides, he doesn't want any old warm body. He wants Amelia Loman with her big heart and bad clothes. Someone like her, at least.

Snow is beginning to fall, and the flakes catch in Maya's whiskers. He wants to take a picture, but he doesn't want to do the thing where you stop to take a picture. 'Whiskers become you,' A.J. tells her.

The compliment to her whiskers sets off a stream of observations about the recital, but A.J. is distracted. 'Maya,' he says, 'do you know how old I am?'

'Yes,' she says. 'Twenty-two.'

'I'm quite a bit older than that.'

'Eighty-nine?'

'I'm ...' He holds up both his palms four times, and then three fingers.

'Forty-three?'

'Good job. I'm forty-three, and in these years I've learned that it's better to have loved and lost and blah blah blah and that it's better to be alone than be with someone you don't really fancy. Do you agree?'

She nods solemnly, and her mouse ears almost fall off.

'Sometimes, though, I get tired of learning lessons.' He looks down at his daughter's puzzled face. 'Are your feet getting wet?'

She nods, and he squats on the ground so that she can get on his back. 'Put your arms around my neck.' Once she is mounted, he stands, groaning a little. 'You're bigger than you used to be.'

She grabs his earlobe. 'What's that?' she asks.

'I used to have an earring,' he says.

'Why?' she asks. 'Were you a pirate?'

'I was young,' he says.

'My age?'

'Older than that. There was a girl.'

'A wench?'

'A woman. She liked this band called The Cure, and she thought it would be cool if she pierced my ear.'

Maya thinks about this. 'Did you have a parrot?'

'I didn't. I had a girlfriend.'

'Could the parrot talk?'

'No, because there wasn't a parrot.'

She tries to trick him. 'What was the parrot's name?'

'There wasn't a parrot.'

'But if there was one, what would his name have been?'

'How do you know it's a he?' he asks.

'Oh!' She puts her hand to her mouth, and she begins to tip backward.

'Hold on to my neck or you'll fall off. Maybe she was called Amy?'

'Amy the parrot. I knew it. Did you have a ship?' Maya asks.

'Yes. It had books on it, and it really was more of a research vessel. We studied a lot.'

'You're ruining this story.'

'It's a fact, Maya. There are murdering kinds of pirates and researching kinds of pirates, and your daddy was the latter.'

*

The island is never a popular destination during the wintertime, but that year Alice is exceptionally inclement. The roads are an ice rink, and the ferry service is cancelled for days at a time. Even Daniel Parish is forced to stay at home. He writes a little, avoids his wife, and spends the rest of his time with A.J. and Maya.

As do most women, Maya likes Daniel. When he comes to the store, he does not talk to her like she is a simpleton just because she is a child. Even at six, she is sensitive to people who are condescending. Daniel always asks her what she is reading and what she thinks. Furthermore, he has bushy blond eyebrows and a voice that makes her think of damask.

One afternoon a week or so after New Year's, Daniel and Maya are reading on the floor of the bookstore when she turns to him and says, 'Uncle Daniel, I have a question. Don't you ever go to work?'

'I'm working right now, Maya,' Daniel says.

She takes off her glasses and wipes them on her shirt. 'You don't look like you're working. You look like you're reading. Don't you have a place you go where you have a job?' She elaborates, 'Lambiase is a police officer. Daddy is a bookseller. What do you do?'

Daniel picks Maya up and carries her to the local-author section of Island Books. Out of courtesy to his brother-in-law, A.J. stocks Daniel's entire body of works, though the only book that ever sells is that first one, *The Children in the Apple Tree*. Daniel points to his name on the spine. 'That's me,' he says. 'That's my job.'

Maya's eyes grow wide. 'Daniel Parish. You write books,'

she says. 'You're a' – she says the word with reverence – 'writer. What is this about?'

'It's about the follies of man. It's a love story and a tragedy.'

'That is very general,' Maya tells him.

'It's about this nurse who has spent her life taking care of other people. She gets in a car accident, and people have to take care of her for the first time in her life.'

'That does not sound like something I would read,' Maya says.

'Bit corny, eh?'

'Nooooo.' She doesn't want to hurt Daniel's feelings. 'But I like books with more action.'

'More action, huh? Me too. The good news is, Miss Fikry, all the time I spend reading, I'm learning how to do it better,' Daniel explains.

Maya thinks about this. 'I want this job.'

'Many people do, my girl.'

'How do I get it?' Maya asks.

'Reading, as aforementioned.'

Maya nods. 'I do that.'

'A good chair.'

'I have one of those.'

'Then you're well on your way,' Daniel tells her before setting her back on the ground. 'I'll teach you the rest later. You're very good company, do you know that?'

'That's what Daddy says.'

'Smart man. Lucky man. Good man. Smart kid, too.'

A.J. calls Maya upstairs to dinner. 'Do you want to join us?' A.J. asks him.

'Bit early for me,' Daniel says. 'Plus I've got work to do.' He winks at Maya.

At last it is March. The roads thaw, turning everything to muck. Ferry service resumes, as do Daniel Parish's wanderings. Sales reps come to town with their summer offerings, and A.J. goes out of his way to be hospitable to them. He takes to wearing a tie as a way of signalling to Maya that he is 'at work' as opposed to 'at home'.

Perhaps because it is the meeting he is most anticipating, he schedules Amelia's sales call for last. About two weeks before their date, he sends her a text: *Pequods OK with you? Or would you rather try something new?*

Queequegs on me this time, she replies. *Did u watch TRUE BLOOD yet?*

The winter had been particularly inhospitable to socializing, so at night, after Maya had gone to sleep, A.J. had plowed through four seasons of *True Blood*. The project hadn't taken him long since he'd liked it more than he expected – a cross between Flannery O'Connor Southern Gothic and *The Fall of the House of Usher* and *Caligula*. He'd been planning to casually dazzle Amelia with his *True Blood* knowledge when she came to town.

You'll have to find out when you get here, he writes, but does not press Send because he decides this text sounds too provocative. He hadn't known when Amelia's wedding was supposed to be, so she could already be a married woman now. *See you next Thursday*, he writes.

On Wednesday, he gets a call from a number he doesn't recognize. The caller turns out to be Brett Brewer,

American Hero, who sounds like Bill from *True Blood*. A.J. thinks the accent sounds fake, but obviously an American Hero would have no need to fake a Southern accent. 'Mr Fikry, Brett Brewer callin' for Amelia. She's had an accident, so she asked me to tell you she'll have to change y'all's meetin' time.'

A.J. loosens his tie. 'I hope nothing serious.'

'I'm always tryin' to get her to stop wearin' those galoshes of hers. They're fine for rain, but kinda dangerous in the ice, y'know? Well, she slipped on some icy steps here in Providence, which is what I told her would happen, and she broke her ankle. She's havin' surgery right now. So nothin' serious, but she'll be laid up for a spell.'

'Give your fiancée my regards, would you?' A.J. says.

A pause. A.J. wonders if the phone has cut out. 'Will do,' Brett Brewer says before hanging up the phone.

A.J. is relieved that Amelia isn't too hurt but a bit disappointed that she isn't coming (and also by the news that the American Hero is most definitely still in the picture).

He thinks about sending Amelia flowers or a book but ultimately decides to send her a text. He tries to find a *True Blood* quote, something that will make her laugh. When he Googles the matter, the quotes all seem too provocative. He writes, *I'm sorry you're hurt. Had been looking forward to hearing Knightley's summer list. Hope we can reschedule soon. Also, and it pains me to say this – 'Giving Jason Stackhouse vampire blood is like giving Ho Hos to a diabetic.'*

Six hours later, Amelia writes back, *YOU WATCHED!!!*
A.J.: *I did.*
Amelia: *Could we do the list over the phone or Skype?*

A.J.: *What's Skype?*

Amelia: *Do I have to teach you everything?!?*

After Amelia explains what Skype is, they decide to meet that way.

A.J. is happy to see her even if it has to be on a video screen. While she's going through the list, he finds he can barely pay attention. He is fascinated by the Amelianess of the things in the frame behind her: a mason jar filled with dying sunflowers, a diploma from Vassar (he thinks it says), a bobblehead of Hermione Granger, a framed picture of a young Amelia and people he guesses are her parents, a lamp with a polka-dotted scarf draped over it, a stapler that looks like a Keith Haring figure, an old edition of some book whose title A.J. cannot make out, a bottle of sparkly nail polish, a wind-up lobster, a set of plastic vampire fangs, an unopened bottle of good champagne, a—

'A.J.,' Amelia interrupts. 'Are you listening?'

'Yes, of course. I'm . . . ' *Staring at your things?* 'I'm unused to Skyping. Can I make Skype a verb?'

'I don't think *OED* has weighed in on the matter, but I think you'll be fine,' she says. 'As I was saying, that Knightley has not one, but two, short-story collections on the summer list.'

Amelia goes on to describe the collections, and A.J. returns to spying. *What is that book?* It's skinnier than a bible or a dictionary. He leans in to try to see it better, but the worn gold-leaf text is too faded to decipher over a video conference call. How irritating that he can't zoom in or change the angle. She is no longer speaking. Clearly, some response is required from A.J.

'Yes, I'm looking forward to reading them,' he says.

'Great. I'll put them in the mail to you today or tomorrow. So that's it until the fall list.'

'I hope you'll be able to come in person.'

'I will. I definitely will.'

'What's the book?' A.J. asks.

'What book?'

'The old one leaning against the lamp, on the table behind you.'

'Wouldn't you like to know?' she says. 'It's my favourite. A gift from my father for my college graduation.'

'So what is it?'

'If you ever make it down to Providence, I'll show you,' she says.

A.J. looks at her. This might have sounded flirtatious except she hadn't even looked up from the notes she'd been writing when she said it. And yet . . .

'Brett Brewer seemed like a nice guy,' A.J. says.

'What?'

'When he called me to say you were hurt and couldn't come,' A.J. explains.

'Right.'

'I thought he sounded like Bill from *True Blood*.'

Amelia laughs. 'Look at you, casually dropping the *True Blood* references. I'll have to tell Brett that the next time I see him.'

'When's the wedding, by the way? Or has it already happened?'

She looks up at him. 'It's off, actually.'

'I'm sorry,' A.J. says.

'It happened a while ago. Over Christmas.'

'I thought because he called . . . '

'He was crashing at my house at the time. I try to stay friends with my exes,' Amelia says. 'I'm that way.'

A.J. knows he is being intrusive, but he can't stop himself. 'What happened?'

'Brett's a great guy, but the sad truth is we didn't have very much in common.'

'Shared sensibility does matter,' A.J. says.

Amelia's phone rings. 'My mother. I have to take this,' she says. 'I'll see you in a couple of months, okay?'

A.J. nods. Skype clicks off, and Amelia's status changes to Away.

He opens his browser and Googles the following phrase: 'educational family attractions near Providence, Rhode Island'. The search yields no distinctive results: a children's museum, a doll museum, a lighthouse, and other things he could more easily do in Boston. He settles on the Green Animals Topiary Garden in Portsmouth. He and Maya had read a picture book with topiary animals in it a while ago, she'd seemed mostly interested in the subject. Plus it's good for them to get off the island, right? He'll take Maya to see the animals, then swing by Providence to see a sick friend.

'Maya,' he says that night at dinner, 'how would you like to see a giant topiary elephant?'

She gives him a look. 'Your voice is funny.'

'It's cool, Maya. You remember that book we read with the topiaries?'

'You mean, when I was little.'

'Right. I found this place with a topiary animal garden. I have to go to Providence anyway to see a sick friend so I thought it would be cool for us to see the animal garden while we were there.' He gets out his computer and shows her the website with the topiary animals.

'Okay,' she says seriously. 'I would like to see that.' She points out that the website says that the topiary garden is in Portsmouth, not Providence.

'Portsmouth and Providence are really close,' A.J. says. 'Rhode Island is the country's smallest state.'

It turns out, however, that Portsmouth and Providence are not all that close. Although there is a bus, the easiest way to get to there is by car, and A.J. doesn't have a driver's licence. He calls Lambiase and asks him to come with them.

'Kid's super into topiaries, huh?' Lambiase asks.

'She's mad for them,' A.J. says.

'Seems a weird thing for a kid to be into, that's all I'm saying.'

'She's a weird kid.'

'But is the middle of winter the best time for touring a garden?'

'It's almost spring. Besides, Maya's into topiaries right now. Who knows if she'll be as interested come summer?'

'Kids change quick. It's true,' Lambiase says.

'Look, you don't have to come.'

'Oh, I'll come. Who wouldn't want to see a giant green elephant? The thing is, though, sometimes people tell you you're on one kind of trip, but it turns out to be another kind of trip, you know what I mean? I just want to know what kind of trip I'm on. Are we going to see topiaries, or are we going to see something else? Maybe that lady friend of yours, say?'

A.J. inhales. 'It crossed my mind that I might stop by to see Amelia, yes.'

A.J. texts Amelia the next day: *Forgot to mention that Maya and I are going to be in Rhode Island next weekend. Instead of you mailing the galleys, I could pick them up.*

Amelia: *Don't have them here. Having them sent from NYC.*

So much for that ill-conceived plan, A.J. thinks.

A couple of minutes later, Amelia sends another text: *What are you doing in Rhode Island anyway?*

A.J.: *Going to the topiary garden in Portsmouth. Maya loves topiaries!* (He is only slightly mortified by that exclamation point.)

Amelia: *Didn't know there was one. Wish I could come with you, but I'm still only semi-mobile.*

A.J. waits a couple of minutes before he texts: *Are you in need of visitors? Maybe we could stop by.*

She does not immediately respond. A.J. takes her silence to mean that she has all the visitors she needs.

The next day, Amelia does text back: *Sure. I'd like that. Don't eat. I'll make something for you and Maya.*

'You can kind of see them if you get on your tippy toes and look over the fence,' A.J. says. 'There in the distance.' They had left Alice at seven that morning, taken the ferry to Hyannis, then driven two hours to Portsmouth only to discover that the Green Animals Topiary Garden is closed from November through May.

A.J. finds that he cannot make eye contact with either his daughter or Lambiase. It is twenty-nine degrees, but shame is keeping him warm.

Maya stands on her toes and when that doesn't work, she tries hopping. 'I can't see anything,' she says.

'Here, I'll get you higher,' Lambiase says, lifting the little girl onto his shoulders.

'Maybe I can see a little bit,' Maya says doubtfully. 'No, I definitely cannot see anything. They're all covered.' Her lower lip begins to quiver. She looks at A.J. with pained eyes. He doesn't think he can take any more of this.

Suddenly, she smiles brightly at A.J. 'But you know what, Daddy? I can imagine what the elephant looks like under the blanket. And the tiger! And the unicorn!' She nods at her father as if to say, *Clearly this imaginative exercise must have been your point in taking me here in the middle of winter.*

'That's very good, Maya.' He feels like the worst parent in the world, but Maya's faith in him seems to be restored.

'Look, Lambiase! The unicorn is shivering. She's glad to be wearing the blanket. Can you see it, Lambiase?'

A.J. walks over to the security kiosk, where the guard shoots him a sympathetic expression. 'Happens all the time,' she says.

'Then you don't think I've scarred my daughter for life?' A.J. asks.

'Sure,' says the guard. 'You've probably done that, but I doubt from anything that happened today. No child ever turned bad from not seeing topiary animals.'

'Even if her father's real purpose was a sexy girl in Providence?'

The guard doesn't seem to hear that part. 'My suggestion to you is that you tour the Victorian residence instead. Kids love old homes.'

'Do they?'

'Some of them. Sure. Why not? Maybe you've got the kind that does.'

At the mansion, Maya is reminded of *From the Mixed-Up Files of Mrs. Basil E. Frankweiler*, a book Lambiase hasn't read.

'Oh, you must, Lambiase,' Maya says. 'You will love it. There's this girl and her brother, and they run away—'

'Running away's no laughing matter.' Lambiase frowns. 'As a police officer, I can tell you that kids don't do well on the streets.'

Maya continues, 'They go to this big museum in New York City, and they hide out there. It's—'

'It's criminal is what it is,' Lambiase says. 'It's definitely trespassing. It's probably breaking and entering, too.'

'Lambiase,' Maya says, 'you are missing the point.'

After an overpriced lunch at the mansion, they drive to Providence to check into their hotel.

'You go visit Amelia,' Lambiase tells A.J. 'I was thinking me and the kid would go to the Children's Museum in town. I'd like to show her the many reasons it would be impractical to hide out in a museum. In a post-September eleventh universe at least.'

'You don't have to do that.' A.J. had planned to take Maya with him so that the visit to Amelia's would seem more casual. (Yes, he was not above using his beloved daughter as a prop.)

'Stop looking guilty,' Lambiase says. 'That's what god-fathers are for. Back-up.'

A.J. gets to Amelia's house just before five. He has brought her an Island Books tote filled with Charlaine Harris novels, a good bottle of Malbec and a bouquet of sunflowers. After he rings the doorbell, he decides the flowers are too obvious and he stows them under the cushions of the porch swing.

When she answers the door, her knee is supported by a wheelie cart. Her cast is pink and has been signed as much as the most popular kid in school's yearbook. She is wearing a navy-blue minidress with a red patterned scarf tied jauntily around her neck. She looks like an airline stewardess.

'Where's Maya?' Amelia asks.

'My friend Lambiase took her to the Providence Children's Museum.'

Amelia cocks her head. 'This isn't a date, is it?'

A.J. tries to explain about the topiary garden having been closed. The story sounds incredibly unconvincing – halfway through telling it, he almost decides to drop the tote and run.

'I'm teasing,' she says. 'Come in.'

Amelia's house is cluttered but clean. She has a purple velvet couch, a smallish grand piano, a dining-room table that seats twelve, many framed pictures of her friends and family, several houseplants in various states of health, a one-eyed tabby cat named Puddleglum, and of course, books everywhere. Her house smells like what she's cooking, which turns out to be lasagne and garlic bread. He takes off his boots so as not to track mud into her house. 'Your place is just like you,' he says.

'Cluttered, mismatched,' she says.

'Eclectic, charming.' He clears his throat and tries not to feel unbearably corny.

They are through with dinner and into their second bottle of wine when A.J. finally gets up the nerve to ask her what had happened with Brett Brewer.

Amelia smiles a little. 'If I tell you the truth, I don't want you to get the wrong idea.'

'I won't. I promise.'

She finishes the dregs of her wine. 'Last fall, when we were corresponding all the time ... Listen, I don't want you to think I broke up with him for you because I didn't. I broke up with him because talking to you made me remember how important it is to share a sensibility with someone, to share passions. I probably sound silly.'

'No,' A.J. says.

She narrows her pretty brown eyes. 'You were so mean to me the first time we met. I still haven't forgiven you, you know.'

'I'd hoped you'd forgotten that.'

'I haven't. My memory is very long, A.J.'

'I was awful,' A.J. says. 'In my defence, I was going through a bad time.' He leans across the table and brushes a blond curl off her face. 'The first time I saw you, I thought you looked like a dandelion.'

She pats her hair self-consciously. 'My hair's such a pain.'

'It's my favourite flower.'

'I think it's technically a weed,' she says.

'You're rather stunning, you know.'

'They used to call me Big Bird in school.'

'I'm sorry.'

'There are worse names,' she says. 'I told my mother about you. She said that you didn't sound like good boyfriend material, A.J.'

'I know. I'm sorry for that. Because I like you enormously.'

Amelia sighs and moves to clear the table.

A.J. rises. 'No, please. Let me. You should sit.' He stacks the dishes and moves them into the dishwasher.

'Do you want to see what that book is?' she says.

'What book?' A.J. asks as he fills the lasagne dish with water.

'The one in my office that you asked about. Isn't that what you came to see?' She rises to her feet, swapping her rolling device for crutches. 'My office is through my bedroom, by the way.'

A.J. nods. He walks briskly through the bedroom so as not to seem presumptuous. He is almost to the office door when Amelia sits on her bed and says, 'Wait. I'll show you the book tomorrow.' She pats the place on the bed next to her. 'My ankle hurts, so apologies if my seduction lacks some of the subtlety it might usually have.'

He tries to be cool as he walks back across the room to Amelia's bed, but A.J. has never been cool.

After Amelia has fallen asleep, A.J. tiptoes into the office.

The book leans against the lamp, unmoved since the day they talked over the computer. Even in person, the cover is too faded to be made out. He opens to the title page: *A Good Man Is Hard to Find and Other Stories* by Flannery O'Connor.

'Dear Amy,' the book is inscribed, 'Mom says this is your favourite writer. I hope you won't mind that I read the title story. I found it a bit dark, but I did enjoy it. A very happy graduation day! I am so proud of you. Love always, Dad.'

A.J. closes the book and sets it back against the lamp.

He writes a note: *Dear Amelia, I honestly don't think I could bear it if you waited until the Knightley fall list to come back to Alice Island. – A.J.F.*

The Celebrated Jumping Frog of Calaveras County

1865/Mark Twain

Proto-postmodernist story of a habitual gambler and his bested frog. The plot isn't much, but it's worth reading because of the fun Twain has with narrative authority. (In reading Twain, I often suspect he is having more fun than I am.)

'Jumping Frog' always reminds me of the time Leon Friedman came to town. Do you remember, Maya? If not, ask Amy to tell you about it some day.

Through the doorway, I can see you both sitting on Amy's old purple couch. You are reading Song of Solomon *by Toni Morrison, and she is reading* Olive Kitteridge *by Elizabeth Strout. The tabby, Puddleglum, is between you, and I am happier than I can ever remember being.*

−A.J.F.

That spring, Amelia takes to wearing flats and finds herself making more sales calls to Island Books than the account, strictly speaking, requires. If her boss notices, he does not say. Publishing is still a gentleperson's business, and besides, A.J. Fikry is carrying an extraordinary number of Knightley titles, more than nearly any other bookstore in the Northeast corridor. The boss does not care whether the numbers are driven by love or commerce or both. 'Perhaps,' the boss says to Amelia, 'you might suggest to Mr Fikry a spotlight on the Knightley Press table in the front of the store?'

That spring, A.J. kisses Amelia just before she gets on the ferry back to Hyannis and says, 'You can't be based from an island. You have to travel too much for your job.'

She holds him at arm's length and laughs at him. 'I agree, but is that your way of asking me to move to Alice?'

'No, I'm ... Well, I'm thinking of you,' A.J. says. 'It wouldn't be practical for you to move to Alice. That's my point.'

'No, it wouldn't be,' she says. She stencils a heart on his chest with a fluorescent pink nail.

'What hue is that?' A.J. asks.

'Rose-Coloured Glasses.' The horn sounds, and Amelia boards the boat.

That spring, while waiting for a Greyhound bus, A.J. says to Amelia, 'You couldn't even get to Alice three months of the year.'

'It would have been easier for me to commute to Afghanistan,' she says. 'I like how you bring this up at the bus station, by the way.'

'I try to put it out of my mind until the last minute.'

'That's one strategy.'

'I take it you mean not a good one.' He grabs her hand. Her hands are large but shapely. A piano player's hands. A sculptress. 'You have the hands of an artist.'

Amelia rolls her eyes. 'And the mind of a book sales rep.'

Her nails are painted a deep shade of purple. 'What colour this time?' he asks.

'Blues Traveler. While I'm thinking about it, would you mind if I painted Maya's nails the next time I'm on Alice? She keeps asking me.'

That spring, Amelia takes Maya to the drugstore and lets her choose any polish colour she likes. 'How do you pick?' Maya says.

'Sometimes I ask myself how I'm feeling,' Amelia says. 'Sometimes I ask myself how I'd like to be feeling.'

Maya studies the rows of glass bottles. She selects a red then puts it back. She takes iridescent silver off the shelf.

'Ooh, pretty. Here's the best part. Each colour has a name,' Amelia tells her. 'Turn the bottle over.'

Maya does. 'It's a title like a book! Pearly Riser,' she reads. 'What's yours called?'

Amy has selected a pale blue. 'Keeping Things Light'.

That weekend, Maya accompanies A.J. to the dock. She throws her arms around Amelia and tells her not to go. 'I don't want to,' Amelia says.

'Then why do you have to?' Maya asks.

'Because I don't live here.'

'Why don't you live here?'

'Because my job is somewhere else.'

'You could come work at the store.'

'I couldn't. Your dad would probably kill me. Besides, I like my job.' She looks at A.J., who is making a great show of checking his phone. The horn sounds.

'Say good-bye to Amy,' A.J. says.

Amelia calls A.J. from the ferry, 'I can't move to Providence. You can't move away from Alice. The situation is pretty much irresolvable.'

'It is,' he agrees. 'What colour were you wearing today?'

'Keeping Things Light.'

'Is that significant?'

'No,' she says.

That spring, Amelia's mother says, 'It isn't fair to you. You're thirty-six years old, and you aren't getting any younger. If you truly want to have a baby, you can't waste any more time in impossible relationships, Amy.'

And Ismay says to A.J., 'It isn't fair to Maya to have this Amelia person be such a big part of your life if you aren't really serious about her.'

And Daniel says to A.J., 'You shouldn't change your life for any woman.'

That June, the good weather makes A.J. and Amelia

forget these and other objections. When Amelia comes to pitch the fall list, she stays for two weeks. She wears seersucker shorts and flip-flops adorned with daisies. 'I probably won't see you much this summer,' she says. 'I'll be travelling for work and then my mother's coming to Providence in August.'

'I could come see you,' A.J. suggests.

'I really won't be around,' Amelia says. 'Except for August, and my mother is an acquired taste.'

A.J. puts sunscreen on her strong, soft back and decides he simply can't be without her. He decides to contrive a reason for her to come to Alice.

The minute she's back in Providence, A.J. calls her on Skype. 'I've been thinking. We should have Leon Friedman come sign at the store in August while the summer people are still in town.'

'You hate the summer people,' Amelia says. She has heard A.J. rant on more than one occasion about the seasonal residents of Alice Island: the families who come into his store right after buying ice cream from Captain Boomer's and let their toddlers run around touching everything, the theatre festival people with their too-loud laughs, the reverse snowbirds who think going to the beach once a week suffices for personal hygiene.

'That isn't true,' A.J. says. 'I like to complain, but I sell them a fair number of books, too. Plus Nic used to say that, contrary to popular belief, the best time to have an author event was during August. The people are so bored by then, they'll do anything for distraction, even go to an author reading.'

'An author reading,' Amelia says. 'My, that is substandard entertainment.'

'Compared to *True Blood*, I suppose.'

She ignores him. 'Actually, I love readings.' When she was starting out in publishing, a boyfriend had dragged her to a ticketed Alice McDermott event at the 92nd Street Y. Amelia thought she hadn't liked *Charming Billy*, but she realized when she heard McDermott read from it – the way her arms moved, the emphasis she placed on certain words – that she hadn't understood the novel at all. When they left the reading, the boyfriend had apologized to her on the subway, 'Sorry if that was kind of a bust.' A week later, she ended the relationship. She can't help thinking how young she'd been, how impossibly high her standards.

'Okay,' Amelia says to A.J. 'I'll put you in touch with the publicist.'

'You'll come, too, right?'

'I'll try. My mother's visiting me in August so—'

'Bring her!' A.J. says. 'I'd like to meet your mother.'

'You only say that because you haven't met her yet,' Amelia says.

'Amelia, my love, you have to attend. I'm having Leon Friedman for you.'

'I don't remember saying I wanted to meet Leon Friedman,' Amelia says. But that's the beauty of video calling, A.J. thinks – he can see that she's smiling.

First thing Monday morning, A.J. calls Leon Friedman's publicist at Knightley. She's twenty-six and brand new like they always are. She has to Google Leon Friedman to figure out what the book is. 'Oh, wow, you're the first appearance request I've had for *The Late Bloomer*.'

'The book is really a store favourite. We've sold quite a few copies of it,' A.J. says.

'You might be the first person to *ever* host an event with Leon Friedman. Like seriously, ever. I'm not sure.' The publicist pauses. 'Let me talk to his editor to see if he's up to doing events. I've never met him, but I'm looking at his picture right now, and he's ... mature. Can I give you a call back?'

'Assuming he's not too mature to travel, I'd want to schedule it for the end of August before the summer people leave. He'll sell more books that way.'

A week later, the publicist leaves word that Leon Friedman is not yet dead and available in August to come to Island Books.

A.J. has not hosted an author for years. The reason being, he has no talent for such arrangements. The last time Island had an author event was back when Nic was still alive, and she had always organized everything. He tries to remember what she had done.

He orders books, hangs posters in the store with Leon Friedman's ancient face, sends relevant social media dispatches, and asks his friends and employees to do the same. Still, his efforts feel incomplete. Nic's book parties always had a gimmick, so A.J. tries to come up with one. Leon Friedman is OLD, and the book flopped. Neither fact seems like much to hang a party on. The book is romantic but incredibly depressing. A.J. decides to call Lambiase. He suggests frozen shrimp from Costco, which

A.J. now recognizes as Lambiase's default party-throwing suggestion. 'Hey,' Lambiase says, 'if you're doing events now, I'd really love to meet Jeffery Deaver. We're all big fans of his at the Alice PD.'

A.J. then calls Daniel, who informs him, 'The only thing a good book party needs is plenty of liquor.'

'Put Ismay on the phone,' A.J. says.

'This isn't terribly literary or brilliant, but how about a garden party?' Ismay says. '*The Late Bloomer*. Blooms, get it?'

'I do,' he says.

'Everyone wears flowered hats. You have the writer judge a hat contest or something. It will lighten the mood, and all the mothers you're friends with will probably show up, if only for the chance to take pictures of each other wearing ridiculous hats.'

A.J. considers this. 'That sounds horrible.'

'It was only a suggestion.'

'But as I think about it, it's probably the right kind of horrible.'

'I accept the compliment. Is Amelia coming?'

'I certainly hope so,' A.J. says. 'I'm having this damned party for her.'

That July, A.J. and Maya go to the only fine jewellery store on Alice Island. A.J. points out a vintage ring with a simple setting and square stone.

'Too plain,' Maya says. She selects a yellow diamond as big as the Ritz, which turns out to be roughly the cost of a first-edition mint-condition *Tamerlane*.

They settle on a 1960s-era ring with a diamond in the

middle and a setting made out of enamel petals. 'Like a daisy,' Maya says. 'Amy likes flowers and happy things.'

A.J. thinks the ring is a bit gaudy, but he knows Maya is right – this is the one Amelia would pick, the one that will make her happy. At the very least, the ring will match her flip-flops.

On the walk back to the bookstore, A.J. warns Maya that Amelia could say no. 'She'd still be our friend,' A.J. says, 'even if she did say no.'

Maya nods, then nods some more. 'Why would she say no?'

'Well . . . Lots of reasons, actually. Your dad is not exactly a catch.'

Maya laughs. 'You're silly.'

'And the place we live is hard to get to, and Amy has to travel for her work.'

'Are you going to ask her at the book party?' Maya asks.

A.J. shakes his head. 'No, I don't want to embarrass her.'

'Why would it embarrass her?'

'I don't want her to feel cornered into saying yes because there's a crowd, you know?' When he had been nine years old, his father had taken him to a Giants game. They had ended up sitting next to a woman who was proposed to at half-time over the Jumbotron. *Yes*, the woman had said when the camera had been on her. But as soon as the third quarter started, the woman had begun to cry uncontrollably. A.J. had never much liked football after that. 'And maybe I don't want to embarrass myself either.'

'After the party?' Maya says.

'Yes, maybe if I work up the courage.' He looks at Maya. 'Is this okay with you, by the way?'

She nods and then she wipes her glasses on her T-shirt. 'Daddy, I told her about the topiaries.'

'What about them exactly?'

'I told her that I don't even like them and that I was pretty sure we had gone to Rhode Island to see her that time.'

'Why did you tell her that?'

'She said a couple of months ago that you were "a hard person to read sometimes".'

'I'm afraid that is probably true.'

Authors never look that much like their author photos, but the first thing A.J. thinks when he meets Leon Friedman is that he *really* doesn't look like his author photo. Photo Leon Friedman is thinner, clean-shaven, and his nose looks longer. Actual Leon Friedman looks somewhere between old Ernest Hemingway and a department store Santa Claus: big red nose and belly, bushy white beard, twinkly eyes. Actual Leon Friedman looks about ten years younger than his author photo. A.J. decides maybe it's just the excess weight and the beard. 'Leon Friedman. Novelist extraordinaire,' Friedman introduces himself. He pulls A.J. into a bear hug. 'Pleased to meet you. You must be A.J. The gal at Knightley Press says you love my book. Good taste on your part, if I do say so myself.'

'It's interesting that you call the book a novel,' A.J. says. 'Would you say it's a novel or a memoir?'

'Ah, well, we'll be debating that until the cows come home, won't we? You wouldn't happen to have a drink for me? A bit of the old vino always makes these kinds of events go better for me.'

Ismay has provided tea and finger sandwiches for the event but not alcohol. The event had been scheduled for 2 p.m. on a Sunday, and Ismay hadn't thought liquor would be necessary or suit the mood of the party. A.J. goes upstairs for a bottle of wine.

When he gets back downstairs, Maya is sitting on Leon Friedman's knee.

'I like *The Late Bloomer,*' Maya is saying, 'but I'm not sure I'm the intended audience.'

'Oh ho ho, that is a very interesting observation, little girl,' Leon Friedman replies.

'I make many of them. The only other writer I know is Daniel Parish. Do you know him?'

'Not sure that I do.'

Maya sighs. 'You are harder to talk to than Daniel Parish. What is your favourite book?'

'Don't know that I have one. Why don't you tell me what you'd like for Christmas instead?'

'Christmas?' Maya says. 'Christmas isn't for four months.'

A.J. claims his daughter from Friedman's lap and gives him a glass of wine in exchange. 'Thank you kindly,' Friedman says.

'Would you mind terribly signing some stock for the store before the reading?' A.J. leads Friedman to the back where he sets him up with a carton of paperback books and a pen. Friedman is about to sign his name on the cover of the book when A.J. stops him. 'We usually have the authors sign on the title page if that's fine with you.'

'Sorry,' Friedman replies, 'I'm new to this.'

'Not at all,' A.J. says.

'Would you mind telling me what kind of show you'd like me to put on out there?'

'Right,' A.J. says. 'I'll say a couple of words about you and then I thought you could introduce the book, say what inspired you to write it and such, then you could maybe read a couple of pages and then perhaps a Q and A with the audience, if there's time. Also, we're having a hat contest in honour of the book, and we'd be honoured if you'd pick the winner.'

'Sounds fantastico,' Friedman says. 'Friedman. F-R-I-E-D-M-A-N,' he says as he signs. 'Easy to forget that I.'

'Is it?' A.J. asks.

'Should be a second *E* there, no?'

Authors are eccentric people so A.J. decides to let this pass. 'You seem comfortable with children,' A.J. says.

'Yeah . . . I often play Santa Claus at the local Macy's at Christmas.'

'Really? That's unusual.'

'I've got a knack for it, I suppose.'

'I mean—' A.J. pauses, trying to decide if what he is about to say will offend Friedman. 'I only mean because you're Jewish.'

'Righto.'

'You make a big point of it in your book. Lapsed Jewish. Is that the correct way of saying it?'

'You can say it any way you want,' Friedman says. 'Say, do you have anything harder than wine?'

Friedman has had a couple of drinks by the time the reading commences, and A.J. supposes this must be the reason the writer garbles several of the longer proper nouns and foreign phrases: Chappaqua, *après moi le déluge*, Hadassah, *L'chaim*, challah, and so on. Some writers aren't comfortable reading aloud. During the Q&A, Friedman keeps his answers brief.

Q: What was it like when your wife died?
A: Sad. Damned sad.
Q: What's your favourite book?
A: The Bible. Or *Tuesdays with Morrie*. Probably the Bible, though.
Q: You look younger than your picture.
A: Why, thank you!
Q: What was it like working at a newspaper?
A: My hands were always dirty.

He's more at home when picking the best hat and during the signing line. A.J.'s managed to get a respectable turnout, and the line extends out the door. 'You should have set up corrals like we do at Macy's,' Friedman suggests.

'Corrals are rarely necessary in my line of work,' A.J. says.

Amelia and her mother are the last to have their books signed.

'It's really great to meet you,' Amelia says. My boyfriend

and I probably wouldn't have gotten together if not for your book.'

A.J. feels for the engagement ring in his pocket. Is this the moment? No, too Jumbotron.

'Give me a hug,' Friedman tells Amelia. She leans over the table, and A.J. thinks he sees the old man look down Amelia's blouse.

'That's the power of fiction for you,' Friedman says.

Amelia studies him. 'I suppose.' She pauses. 'Only it isn't fiction, right? It really happened.'

'Yes, sweetheart, of course,' Friedman says.

A.J. interrupts. 'Perhaps, Mr Friedman meant to say that *that* is the power of narrative.'

Amelia's mother, who is the size of a grasshopper and has the personality of a praying mantis, says, 'Perhaps Mr Friedman is trying to say that a relationship based on loving a book is not likely to be much of a relationship.' Amelia's mother, then, offers her hand to Mr Friedman. 'Margaret Loman. My spouse died a couple of years ago, too. Amelia, my daughter, made me read your book for my Widows of Charleston Book Club. Everyone thought it was marvellous.'

'Oh, how nice. How ... ' Friedman smiles brightly at Mrs Loman. 'How ... '

'Yes?' Mrs Loman repeats.

Friedman clears his throat, then wipes sweat from his brow and nose. Flushed, he looks even more like Santa Claus. He opens his mouth as if to speak, then throws up all over the pile of just signed stock and Amelia's mother's beige Ferragamo pumps. 'I seem to have had too much to drink,' Friedman says. He belches.

'Obviously,' says Mrs Loman.

'Mom, A.J.'s apartment is up here.' Amelia points her mother toward the stairs.

'He lives above the store?' Mrs Loman asks. 'You never mentioned that delightful piece of—' At that moment, Mrs Loman slips in the rapidly expanding vomit puddle. She rights herself, but her hat, which had taken honourable mention, is a lost cause.

Friedman turns to A.J. 'Apologies, sir. I seem to have had too much to drink. A cigarette and some fresh air some-times settles my stomach. If someone could point me outside . . . ' A.J. leads Friedman out the back way.

'What happened?' Maya asks. Once the Friedman talk had turned out not to be to her interests, she had turned her attentions back to *The Lightning Thief*. She walks over to the signing table and, upon seeing the throw-up, vomits herself.

Amelia rushes to Maya's side. 'Are you all right?'

'I did not expect to see that there,' Maya says.

Meanwhile, in the alley to the side of the store, Leon Friedman is throwing up again.

'Do you think maybe you have food poisoning?' A.J. asks.

Friedman doesn't answer.

'Maybe it was the ferry ride that did it? Or all the excite-ment? The heat?' A.J. doesn't know why he feels the need to talk so much. 'Mr Friedman, perhaps I can get you something to eat?'

'You got a lighter?' Friedman says hoarsely. 'I left mine in my bag inside.'

A.J. runs back in the store. He can't find Friedman's bag. 'I NEED A LIGHTER!' he yells. He rarely raises his voice. 'Seriously, does anyone work here who can get me a lighter?'

But everyone is gone, aside from a clerk, who's occupied at the cash register, and a couple of stragglers from the Friedman signing. A smartly dressed woman of about Amelia's age opens her capacious leather handbag. 'I might have one.'

A.J. stands there, seething while the woman searches through the purse, which is really more like luggage. He thinks that this is why one shouldn't let authors into the store. The woman comes up empty-handed. 'Sorry,' she says. 'I quit smoking after my father died of emphysema, but I thought I might still have the lighter.'

'No, it's fine. I have one upstairs.'

'Is something wrong with the writer?' the woman asks.

'The usual,' A.J. says, heading up the stairs.

In his apartment, he finds Maya by herself. Her eyes look moist. 'I threw up, Daddy.'

'I'm sorry.' A.J. locates the lighter in his drawer. He slams the drawer shut. 'Where's Amelia?'

'Are you going to propose?' Maya asks.

'No, darling. Not at this particular moment. I've got to deliver a lighter to an alcoholic.'

She considers this information. 'Can I come with you?' she asks.

A.J. puts the lighter in his pocket and, for expediency, scoops up Maya, who really is too big to be carried.

They go down the stairs and through the bookstore

and outside to where A.J. had left Friedman. Friedman's head is haloed by smoke. The pipe, which droops languorously from his fingers, makes a curious bubbling sound.

'I couldn't find your bag,' A.J. says.

'Had it with me all along,' Friedman says.

'What kind of pipe is that?' Maya asks. 'I have never seen a pipe like that before.'

A.J.'s first impulse is to cover Maya's eyes, but then he laughs. Had Friedman actually travelled on the plane with drug paraphernalia? He turns to his daughter. 'Maya, do you remember when we read *Alice's Adventures in Wonderland* last year?'

'Where's Friedman?' Amelia asks.

'Passed out in the backseat of Ismay's SUV,' A.J. replies.

'Poor Ismay.'

'She's used to it. She's been Daniel Parish's media escort for years.' A.J. makes a face. 'I think the decent thing would be for me to go with them.' The plan had been for Ismay to drive Friedman to the ferry and then the airport, but A.J. can't do that to his sister-in-law.

Amelia kisses him. 'Good man. I'll watch Maya and clean up here,' she says.

'Thank you. It sucks, though,' A.J. says. 'Your last night in town.'

'Well,' she says, 'at least it was memorable. Thanks for bringing Leon Friedman even if he's a bit different than I imagined him.'

'Just a bit.' He kisses Amelia then furrows his brow. 'I

thought this was going to be more romantic than it turned out to be.'

'It was very romantic. What's more romantic than a lecherous old drunk looking down my blouse?'

'He's more than a drunk . . .' A.J. mimes the universal gesture for toking up.

'Maybe he has cancer or something?' Amelia says.

'Maybe . . .'

'At least he waited until the event was over,' she says.

'And I, for one, think the event was the worse for it,' A.J. says.

Ismay honks the car horn.

'That's me,' A.J. says. 'Do you really have to spend the night at the hotel with your mother?'

'I don't have to. I am a grown woman, A.J.,' Amelia says. 'It's just that we're leaving early for Providence tomorrow.'

'I don't think I made a very good impression,' A.J. says.

'No one does,' she says. 'I wouldn't worry about it.'

'Well, wait up for me, if you can.' Ismay honks the horn again, and A.J. runs to the car.

Amelia begins cleaning up the bookstore. She starts with the vomit and has Maya round up less objectionable detritus like flower petals and plastic cups. In the back row sits the woman who hadn't had a lighter. She wears a floppy grey fedora and a silky maxi-dress. Her clothes look like they could be from a thrift shop, but Amelia, who actually shops in thrift stores, recognizes them as expensive. 'Were you here for the reading?' Amelia asks.

'Yes,' the woman says.

'What did you think?' Amelia asks.

'He was very animated,' the woman says.

'Yes, that's true.' Amelia squeezes a sponge into a bucket. 'I can't say he was completely what I was expecting.'

'What were you expecting?' the woman asks.

'Someone more intellectual, I think. That sounds snobby. Maybe that's not the right word. Someone wiser maybe.'

The woman nods. 'No, I can see that.'

'My expectations were probably too high. I work for his publisher. It was my favourite thing I ever sold, actually.'

'Why was it your favourite?' the woman asks.

'I . . . ' Amelia looks at the woman. She has kind eyes. Amelia has often been fooled by kind eyes. 'I had lost my father not long before, and I guess something in the voice reminded me of him. Also, there were so many true, true things in it.' Amelia moves on to sweeping the floor.

'Am I in your way?' the woman asks.

'No, you're fine where you are.'

'I feel bad just watching you,' the woman says.

'I like sweeping, and you're dressed too nicely to help.' Amelia sweeps the room in long, rhythmic strokes.

'They make the publisher clean up after readings?' the woman asks.

Amelia laughs. 'No. I'm the bookstore owner's girlfriend, too. I'm helping out for the day.'

The woman nods. 'He must have been a huge fan of the book to bring Leon Friedman here after all these years.'

'Yes.' Amelia lowers her voice to a whisper. 'The truth is, he did it for me. It was the first book we loved together.'

'That's cute. Kind of like the first restaurant you go to or the first song you danced to or something.'

'Exactly.'

'Maybe he's planning to propose to you?' the woman says.

'The thought had crossed my mind.'

Amelia empties the dustpan into the garbage can.

'Why don't you think the book sold?' the woman asks after a bit.

'*The Late Bloomer?* Well ... because it's competitive out there. And even when a book is good, sometimes it still doesn't work.'

'That must be hard,' the woman says.

'Are you writing a book or something?'

'I've tried, yes.'

Amelia pauses to look at the woman. She has long brown hair, well cut and super-straight. Her purse probably cost as much as Amelia's car. Amelia holds out her hand to introduce herself to the woman. 'Amelia Loman.'

'Leonora Ferris.'

'Leonora. Like Leon,' Maya pipes up. She has had a milkshake and is now recovered. 'I am Maya Fikry.'

'Are you from Alice?' Amelia asks Leonora.

'No, I came in for the day. For the reading.'

Leonora stands, and Amelia folds her chair and sets it by the wall.

'You must be a big fan of the book, too,' Amelia says. 'Like I said before, my boyfriend lives here, and I know from experience that Alice isn't the easiest place in the world to get to.'

'No, it isn't,' Leonora says as she picks up her handbag.

All at once, Amelia is struck with a thought. She turns around and calls, 'No one travels without purpose. Those who are lost wish to be lost.'

'You're quoting *The Late Bloomer*,' Leonora says after a long pause. 'It really was your favourite.'

'It was,' Amelia says. '"When I was young, I never felt young." Something like that. Do you remember the rest of the quote?'

'No,' Leonora says.

'Writers don't remember everything they write,' Amelia says. 'How could they?'

'Nice talking to you.' Leonora starts heading for the door.

Amelia puts her hand on Leonora's shoulder.

'You're him, aren't you?' Amelia says. 'You're Leon Friedman.'

Leonora shakes her head. 'Not truly.'

'What does that mean?'

'A long time ago, a girl wrote a novel, and she tried to sell it, but no one wanted it. It was about an old man who lost his wife, and it didn't have supernatural beings in it or a high concept to speak of, and so she thought it would be easier if she retitled the book and called it a memoir.'

'That's . . . That's . . . wrong,' Amelia stammers.

'No, it isn't. All the things in it are still emotionally true even if they aren't literally so.'

'So who was that man?'

'I called a casting office. He usually plays Santa.'

Amelia shakes her head. 'I don't understand. Why do

the reading? Why go to the expense and bother? Why risk it?'

'The book had already flopped. And sometimes you want to know ... to see for yourself that your work has meant something to someone.'

Amelia studies Leonora. 'I feel a little fooled,' she says finally. 'You're a good writer, you know?'

'I do know,' Leonora says.

Leonora Ferris disappears down the street and Amelia goes back into the store.

Maya says to her, 'It has been a very weird day.'

'I agree.'

'Who was that woman, Amy?' Maya asks.

'Long story,' Amelia tells her.

Maya makes a face.

'She was distantly related to Mr Friedman,' Amelia says.

Amelia gets Maya into bed then pours herself a drink and debates whether or not to tell A.J. about Leonora Ferris. She doesn't want to sour him on the idea of author events. She also doesn't want to make herself look foolish in his eyes or compromise herself professionally: she has sold him a book that has now revealed itself to be a fake. And maybe Leonora Ferris is right. Maybe it doesn't matter if the book is, strictly speaking, true. She thinks back to a sophomore seminar she had taken in literary theory. *What is true?* the teaching fellow would ask them. *Aren't memoirs constructions anyway?* She would always fall asleep during this class, which was embarrassing because only nine people were in it. All these years later, Amelia finds she can still drift off to the memory.

A.J. arrives back at the apartment a little after ten. 'How was the drive?' Amelia asks.

'The best thing I can say is that Friedman was passed out for most of it. I've spent the last twenty minutes cleaning Ismay's backseat,' A.J. reports.

'Well, I certainly look forward to your next author event, Mr Fikry,' Amelia says.

'Was it that much of a disaster?'

'No. I think everyone had a great time, actually. And the store did sell a lot of books.' Amelia stands to leave. If she doesn't leave now, she won't be able to resist telling A.J. about Leonora Ferris. 'I should get back to the hotel. Since we're leaving so early tomorrow.'

'No, wait. Stay a bit.' A.J. feels for the jewellery box in his pocket. He doesn't want the summer to end without having asked her, come what may. He is about to miss his moment. He plucks the box from his pocket and throws it at her. 'Think quick,' he says.

'What?' she says as she turns. The jewellery box hits her smack in the middle of the forehead. 'Ow. What the fuck, A.J.?'

'I was trying to get you not to leave. I thought you'd catch it. I'm sorry.' He goes over to her and kisses her on the head.

'You threw a little high.'

'You're taller than me. I sometimes overestimate by how much.'

She picks up the box from the floor and opens it.

'It's for you,' A.J. says. 'It's . . . ' He gets down on one knee, clasps her hand between his, and tries not to feel

phoney, like an actor in a play. 'Let's get married,' he says
with an almost pained expression. 'I know I'm stuck on this
island, that I'm poor, a single father, and in a business with
somewhat diminishing returns. I know that your mother
hates me, that I'm quite obviously crap when it comes to
hosting author events.'

'This is an odd proposal,' she says. 'Lead with your
strong stuff, A.J.'

'All I can say is ... All I can say is we'll figure it out, I
swear. When I read a book, I want you to be reading it at
the same time. I want to know what Amelia would think of
it. I want you to be mine. I can promise you books and conversation and all my heart, Amy.'

She knows that what he says is true. He is, for the reasons
he's said, a terrible match for her or anybody else, for that
matter. The travel is going to be murder. This man, this
A.J., is prickly and argumentative. He thinks he is never
wrong. Maybe he never *is* wrong.

But he had been wrong. Infallible A.J. had not sniffed out
Leon Friedman as a fraud. She's not sure why this matters
at this moment, but it does. Maybe it is evidence of some
boyish, delusional part of him. She cocks her head. *I will
keep this secret because I love you.* As Leon Friedman (Leonora
Ferris?) once wrote, 'A good marriage is, at least, one part
conspiracy.'

She furrows her brow, and A.J. thinks she is going to say
no. 'A good man is hard to find,' she says finally.

'Do you mean the O'Connor story? The one on your
desk. It's an awfully dark thing to bring up at a time like
this.'

'No, I mean you. I've been looking for ever. It was only two trains and a boat away.'

'You can skip some of the trains if you drive,' A.J. tells her.

'And what would you know about driving?' Amelia asks.

The next fall, just after the leaves have turned, Amelia and A.J. get married.

Lambiase's mother, who has come as his date, says to her son, 'I like all weddings, but isn't it particularly lovely when two grown-ups decide to get married?' Lambiase's mother would like to see her son remarry some day.

'I know what you mean, Ma. Doesn't seem like they're going in with their eyes closed,' Lambiase says. 'He knows she isn't perfect. She knows he definitely isn't perfect. They know there's no such thing as perfect.'

Maya has chosen to be ring bearer because the job has more responsibility than flower girl. 'If you lose a flower, you get another flower,' Maya reasons. 'If you lose the ring, everyone is sad for ever. The ring bearer has much more power.'

'You sound like Gollum,' A.J. says.

'Who's Gollum?' Maya wants to know.

'Someone very nerdy that your father likes,' Amelia says.

Before the service, Amelia gives Maya a present: a small box of bookplates that read THIS BOOK BELONGS TO MAYA TAMERLANE FIKRY.' At this stage in her life, Maya is fond of things with her name on them.

'I'm glad we're going to be related,' Amelia says. 'I really like you, Maya.'

Maya is occupied with pasting her first bookplate into the book she's currently reading, *The Astonishing Life of Octavian Nothing*. 'Yeah,' she says. 'Oh, wait.' She takes a bottle of orange nail polish from her pocket. 'For you.'

'I don't have any orange,' Amelia says. 'Thank you.'

'I know. That's why I picked it.'

Amy turns the bottle over and reads the bottom: *A Good Man-darin Is Hard to Find*.

A.J. had suggested inviting Leon Friedman to the wedding, an idea Amelia rejects. They do agree on a passage from *The Late Bloomer* to be read at the service by one of Amelia's college friends.

'It is the secret fear that we are unlovable that isolates us,' the passage goes, 'but it is only because we are isolated that we think we are unlovable. Someday, you do not know when, you will be driving down a road. And someday, you do not know when, he, or indeed she, will be there. You will be loved because for the first time in your life, you will truly not be alone. You will have chosen to not be alone.'

None of Amelia's other college friends recognize the woman who is reading the passage, but none of them find this particularly odd either. Vassar is a small college, though certainly not the kind of place where everyone can know everyone, and Amelia has always had a knack for making friends with people from a variety of social circles.

The Girls in Their Summer Dresses

1939/Irwin Shaw

Man watches women besides his wife. The wife doesn't approve. Lovely twist, more like a turn, at the end. You're a good reader, and you'll probably see it coming. (Is a twist less satisfying if you know it's coming? Is a twist that you can't predict symptomatic of bad construction? These are things to consider when writing.)

Not particularly apropos of writing but . . . Someday, you may think of marrying. Pick someone who thinks you're the only person in the room.

—A.J.F.

Ismay waits in the foyer of her house. Her legs are crossed so that one foot is wrapped around the calf of her other leg. She once saw an anchorwoman sit that way, and it had impressed her. A woman needs skinny legs and flexible knees to accomplish it. She wonders if the dress she's picked for the day will be too light. The material is silk, and summer is over.

She looks at her phone. It's 11 a.m., which means the ceremony will have already begun. Perhaps she should leave without him?

As she is already late, she decides that there is no point in going alone. If she waits, she can yell at him when he arrives. She finds pleasure where she can.

Daniel comes through the door at 11:26. 'Sorry,' he says. 'A few of the kids from my class wanted to go for a drink. One thing led to another, you know how it is.'

'Yes,' she says. She doesn't feel like yelling any more. Silence will be better.

'I crashed in my office. My back is killing me.' He kisses her on the cheek. 'You look fantastic.' He whistles. 'You still have great legs, Izzie.'

'Get changed,' she says. 'You smell like a liquor store. Did you drive here yourself?'

'I'm not drunk. I'm hung over. Be precise, Ismay.'

'It's amazing you're still alive,' she says.

'Probably so,' he says as he goes up the stairs.

'Would you grab my wrap when you come back down?' she says, but she isn't sure if he has heard her.

The wedding is, as weddings are, as weddings will always be, Ismay thinks. A.J. looks sloppy in his blue seersucker suit. Couldn't he have rented a tuxedo? It's Alice Island, not the Jersey shore. And where had Amelia gotten that awful Renaissance Faire dress? It's more yellow than white, and she looks hippy in it. She's always wearing vintage clothes and she doesn't exactly have the right body type for them. Who's she kidding with those big gerbera in her hair – she's not twenty, for God's sake. When she smiles, she's all gums.

When did I get so negative? Ismay wonders. Their happiness is not her unhappiness. Unless it is. What if there is only an equal ratio of happiness to unhappiness in the world at any given time? She should be nicer. It's a well-known fact that hate shows up on your face once you're forty. Besides, Amelia is attractive, even if she isn't beautiful like Nic. Look how much Maya is smiling. Lost another tooth. And A.J. is so happy. Watch that lucky bastard try not to cry.

Ismay *is* happy for A.J., whatever that means, but the wedding itself is a trial. The event makes her younger sister seem even deader and also leads to unwanted reflection on her sundry disappointments. She is forty-four years old. She is married to a too-handsome man, whom she no longer loves. She has had seven miscarriages in the last dozen years. She is, according to her gynaecologist, in perimenopause: *So much for that.*

She looks across the venue at Maya. What a pretty girl

she is, and she's smart, too. Ismay waves to her, but Maya has her head in a book and she doesn't seem to notice. The little girl has never particularly warmed to Ismay, which everyone thinks is odd. In general, Maya prefers adult company, and Ismay has a reputation for being good with children after having taught them for the last twenty years. *Twenty years. Jesus.* Without even noticing it, she has gone from the bright new teacher whose legs all the boys stare at to old Mrs Parish who does the school play. They think it's silly how much she cares about these productions. Of course, they are overestimating her investment. How many years can she be expected to go on, one mediocre production blending in with the next? Different faces, but none of these kids ever turns out to be Meryl Streep.

Ismay pulls her wrap tighter around her shoulders and decides to take a walk. She heads down the pier then takes off her kitten heels and walks across the beach, which is empty. It is late September, and the air feels like fall. She tries to remember the name of the book where the woman swims out to sea and kills herself in the end.

It would be so easy, Ismay thinks. You walk out. You swim for a while. You swim too far. You don't try to swim back. Your lungs fill up. It hurts for a bit, but then it's over. Nothing ever hurts again, and your conscience is clear. You don't leave a mess. Maybe your body washes up some day. Maybe it doesn't. Daniel wouldn't even look for her. Maybe he would look for her, but he certainly wouldn't look very hard.

Of course! The book is *The Awakening* by Kate Chopin. How she had loved that novel (novella?) at seventeen.

Maya's mother had ended her life in the same fashion, and Ismay wonders, not for the first time, if Marian Wallace had read *The Awakening*. She has thought a lot about Marian Wallace over the years.

Ismay walks into the water, which is even colder than she thought it would be. *I can do this*, she thinks. Just keep walking.

I may just do this.

'Ismay!'

Despite herself, Ismay turns. It's Lambiase, that annoying cop friend of A.J.'s. He is carrying her shoes.

'Cold for a swim?'

'A little,' she replies. 'I came out here to clear my head.'

Lambiase walks over to her. 'Sure.'

Ismay's teeth are chattering, and Lambiase takes off his suit coat and puts it over her shoulders. 'Must be hard,' Lambiase says. 'Seeing A.J. married to someone other than your sister.'

'Yes. Amelia seems lovely, though.' Ismay begins to cry, but the sun has mostly set and she is not sure if Lambiase can see it.

'The thing about weddings,' he says, 'is that they can make a person feel lonely as hell.'

'Yes.'

'I hope I'm not out of line here and I know we don't know each other that well. But, well, your husband's an idiot. If I had a nice-looking professional woman like you—'

'You *are* out of line.'

'I'm sorry,' Lambiase says. 'I got no manners.'

Ismay nods. 'I wouldn't say you have no manners,' she says. 'You did lend me your coat. Thank you for that.'

'Fall comes fast on Alice,' Lambiase says. 'We should go back inside.'

Daniel is talking up Amelia's maid of honour by the bar under Pequod's whale, which has been wrapped with Christmas lights for the occasion. Janine, a Hitchcock blonde in glasses, came up through the publishing ranks with Amelia. Daniel doesn't know this, but Janine has been given the task of making sure the great writer doesn't get out of line.

For the wedding, Janine is wearing a yellow gingham dress that Amelia had picked out and paid for. 'I know you'll never wear this again,' Amelia had said.

'Hard colour to pull off,' Daniel says. 'But you look great in it. Janine, right?'

She nods.

'Janine the maid of honour. Should I ask you what you do?' Daniel says. 'Or is that boring party talk?'

'I'm an editor,' she says.

'Sexy and smart. What are your books?'

'A picture book I edited about Harriet Tubman was a Caldecott Honor Book a couple of years ago.'

'Impressive,' Daniel says, though in fact he is disappointed. He is on the hunt for a new publishing home. His sales aren't what they once were, and he believes the people at his old publisher aren't doing enough for him. He'd like to leave them before they leave him. 'That's the top prize, right?'

'It didn't win. It got an honour.'

'I bet you're a good editor,' he says.

'Based on what?'

'Well, you wouldn't let me think your book won when it was only a runner-up.'

Janine looks at her watch.

'Janine looks at her watch,' Daniel says. 'She is bored with the old writer.'

Janine smiles. 'Strike the second sentence. Reader will know. Show, don't tell.'

'If you're going to say things like that, I need a drink.' Daniel signals the bartender. 'Vodka. Grey Goose, if you have it. And a little seltzer.' He turns to Janine. 'For you?'

'Glass of rosé.'

'"Show, don't tell" is a complete crock of shit, Janine the maid of honour,' Daniel lectures her. 'It comes from Syd Field's screenplay books, but it doesn't have a thing to do with novel writing. Novels are all tell. The best ones at least. Novels aren't meant to be imitation screenplays.'

'I read your book when I was in junior high,' Janine says.

'Oh, don't tell me that. It makes me feel ancient.'

'It was my mom's favourite.'

Daniel pantomimes getting shot through the heart. Ismay taps him on the shoulder. 'I'm going home,' she whispers in his ear.

Daniel follows her out to the car. 'Ismay, hold up.'

Ismay drives because Daniel is too drunk to drive. They live in the Cliffs, the most expensive part of Alice Island. All the houses have views, and the road that leads to them is uphill, twisty with many blind spots, poorly lit, and lined with yellow signs imploring caution.

'You took that turn a little fast, darling,' Daniel says.

She thinks about driving them both off the road and into the ocean, and the thought makes her happy, happier than she would have been if she'd only killed herself. She realizes in that moment that she doesn't want to be dead. She wants Daniel to be dead. Or at least gone. Yes, gone. She'd settle for gone.

'I don't love you any more.'

'Ismay, you're being absurd. You always get like this at weddings.'

'You are not a good man,' Ismay says.

'I'm complex. And maybe I'm not good, but I'm certainly not the worst. It's no reason to end a perfectly average marriage,' Daniel says.

'You're the grasshopper, and I'm the ant. And I'm tired of being the ant.'

'That's a rather juvenile reference. I'm sure you can do better.'

Ismay pulls the car over to the side of the road. Her hands are shaking.

'You are bad. And what's worse is, you've made me bad,' she says.

'I don't know what you're talking about.' A car whizzes by them, close enough to rattle the sides of the SUV. 'Ismay, this is an insane place to park. If you want to argue, let's drive home and do it properly.'

'Every time I see her with A.J. and Amelia, I'm sick. She should be ours.'

'What?'

'Maya,' Ismay says. 'If you'd done the right thing, she'd be ours. But you, you can never do anything hard. And I let you be that way.'

She looks steadily at Daniel. 'I know that Marian Wallace was your girlfriend.'

'That isn't true.'

'Don't lie! I know that she came here to kill herself in your front yard. I know that she left Maya for you, but you either were too lazy or too much of a coward to claim her.'

'If you thought that was true, why didn't you do something?' Daniel asks.

'Because it isn't my job! I was pregnant, and it wasn't my responsibility to clean up after your affairs.'

Another car speeds past, nearly sideswiping them.

'But if you'd been brave and come to me, I would have adopted her, Daniel. I would have forgiven you and I would have taken her in. I waited for you to say something, but you never did. I waited for days, then weeks, then years.'

'Ismay, you can believe what you want, but Marian Wallace was not my girlfriend. She was a fan who came to a reading.'

'How stupid do you think I am?'

Daniel shakes his head. 'She was a girl who came to a reading, and a girl I slept with once. How could I even be sure the child was mine?' He tries to take Ismay's hand, but she pulls away.

'It's funny,' Ismay says. 'Every last bit of love I had for you is gone.'

'I still love you,' Daniel says. At that moment headlights catch the rearview mirror.

The hit comes from behind, knocking the car into the centre of the road so that it is crossing both lanes of traffic.

'I think I'm okay,' Daniel says. 'Are you okay?'

'My leg,' she says. 'It might be broken.'

More headlights, this time from the opposite side of the road. 'Ismay, you have to drive.' He turns in time to see the truck. A twist, he thinks.

In the first chapter of Daniel's famous first novel, the main character is in a catastrophic car accident. Daniel had struggled with the section, because it occurred to him that everything he knew about horrible car accidents had come from books he'd read and movies he'd seen. The description he finally settled on, after what must have been fifty passes, never much satisfied him. A series of fragments in the style of modernist poets. Apollinaire or Breton, maybe, but not nearly as good as either.

Lights, bright enough to dilate her eyes.
Horns, flaccid and come too late.
Metal crumpling like tissue.
The body was not in pain but only because the body was gone, elsewhere.

Yes, Daniel thinks just after impact but before death, *like that.* The passage hadn't been as bad as he had thought.

PART II

A Conversation with My Father

1972/Grace Paley

Dying father argues with daughter about the 'best' way to tell a story. You'll love this, Maya, I'm sure. Maybe I'll go downstairs and push it into your hands right now.

– A.J.F.

The assignment for Maya's creative-writing class is to tell a story about someone you wish you knew better. *My biological father is a ghost to me*, she writes. She thinks the first sentence is good, but where to go from there? After 250 words and a whole morning wasted, she concedes defeat. There's no story because she doesn't know anything about the man. He truly is a ghost to her. The failure was in the conception.

A.J. brings her a grilled cheese sandwich. 'How's it going, Hemingway?'

'Don't you ever knock?' she says. She accepts the sandwich and shuts the door. She used to love living above the store, but now that she is fourteen and Amelia lives there, too, the apartment feels small. And noisy. She can hear customers downstairs all day. How is a person to write under such conditions?

Out of desperation, Maya writes about Amelia's cat.

Puddleglum never imagined he'd move from Providence to Alice Island.

She revises, *Puddleglum never imagined he'd live in a bookstore.*

Gimmicky, she decides. That's what Mr Balboni, the creative-writing teacher, will say. She has already written a story from the point of view of the rain and the point of view of a very old library book. 'Interesting concepts,' Mr Balboni had written on the library book story, 'but you might want to try writing about a human character next time. Do you really want anthropomorphizing to become your thing?'

She had had to look up 'anthropomorphize' before deciding that, no, she didn't want it to become her thing. She doesn't want to have *a thing*. And yet can she be blamed if it kind of is her thing? Her childhood had been spent reading books and imagining lives for customers and sometimes for inanimate objects like the teapot or the bookmark carousel. It had not been a lonely childhood, though many of her intimates had been somewhat less than real.

A little later, Amelia knocks. 'Are you working? Can you take a break?'

'Come in,' Maya says.

Amelia flops onto the bed. 'What are you writing?'

'I don't know. That's the problem. I thought I had an idea, but it didn't work.'

'Oh, that *is* a problem.'

Maya explains the assignment. 'It's supposed to be about someone important to you. Someone who died, probably, or someone you wish you knew better.'

'Maybe you could write about your mother?'

Maya shakes her head. She doesn't want to hurt Amelia's feelings, but that seems kind of obvious. 'I know as little about her as I do my biological father,' she says.

'You lived with her for two years. You know her name and some of her backstory. That might be a place to start.'

'I know as much as I want to know about her. She had chances. She screwed everything up.'

'That isn't true,' Amelia says.

'She gave up, didn't she?'

'She probably had reasons. I'm sure she did the best she could.' Amelia's mother had died two years ago, and though their relationship had been challenging at times, she misses her with an unexpected ferocity. For instance, until her death, her mother had sent her new underwear in the mail every other month. Amelia had not once had to buy underwear her whole life. Recently, she had found herself standing in the lingerie department at TJ Maxx, and as she went through the panty bin, she had begun to cry: *No one will ever love me that much again.*

'Someone who died?' A.J. says over dinner. 'What about Daniel Parish? You were good friends with him.'

'When I was a child,' Maya says.

'Isn't he why you decided to be a writer?' A.J. says.

Maya rolls her eyes. 'No.'

'She had a crush on him when she was little,' A.J. says to Amelia.

'Da-ad! That isn't true.'

'Your first literary crush is a big deal,' Amelia says. 'Mine was John Irving.'

'You lie,' A.J. says. 'It was Ann M. Martin.'

Laughing, Amelia pours herself another glass of wine. 'Yeah, probably right.'

'I'm glad you both think this is so funny,' Maya says. 'I'm probably going to fail and then I'll probably end up just like my mother.' She stands up from the table and runs to her room. Their apartment is not built for dramatic exits, and she bangs her knee on a bookshelf. 'This place is too small,' she says.

She stalks into her room and slams the door.

'Should I go after her?' A.J. whispers.

'No. She needs space. She's a teenage girl. Let her stew for a bit.'

'Maybe she's right,' A.J. says. 'This place *is* too small.'

They have been browsing houses online for as long as they've been married. Now that Maya is a teenager, the attic apartment with its one bathroom has shrunk exponentially, magically. Half the time, A.J. finds himself using the public store bathroom to avoid competing with Maya and Amelia. Customers are more civilized than these two. Besides, business has been good (or at least stable), and if they moved, he could use the apartment for an expanded Children's section with a story-time area, or maybe gifts and greeting cards.

In their price range on Alice Island, all the houses are starter homes, though A.J. feels like he is past the starter-home age of his life. Weird kitchens and floorplans, too-small rooms, ominous references to foundation issues. Until the housing search began, A.J. could count on one hand the number of times he had thought about *Tamerlane* with any sort of regret.

Later that night, Maya finds a slip of paper under her door:

Maya,
If you're stuck, reading helps:
'The Beauties' by Anton Chekhov, 'The Doll's House' by
Katherine Mansfield, 'A Perfect Day for Bananafish' by J. D.
Salinger, 'Brownies' or 'Drinking Coffee Elsewhere' both by
ZZ Packer, 'In the Cemetery Where Al Jolson Is Buried' by

Amy Hempel, 'Fat' by Raymond Carver,' 'Indian Camp' by
Ernest Hemingway.
We should have them all downstairs. Just ask if you can't
find anything, though you know where everything is better
than I.
Love,
Dad

She stuffs the list in her pocket and walks downstairs,
where the store is closed for the night. She spins the bookmark carousel – *Why, hello there, carousel!* – and makes a sharp
right turn into Adult Fiction.

Maya is nervous and a little excited when she hands the
story to Mr Balboni.

'"A Trip to the Beach",' he says, reading the title.

'It's from the point of view of sand,' Maya says. 'It's
winter on Alice, and the sand misses the tourists.'

Mr Balboni shifts, and his tight black leather pants
squeak. He encourages them to emphasize the positive
while at the same time reading with a critical and ideally
informed eye. 'Well, that sounds like it has evocative
description already.'

'I'm kidding, Mr Balboni. I'm trying to move away from
anthropomorphizing.'

'I'll look forward to reading it,' Mr Balboni says.

The next week, Mr Balboni announces that he's going to
read a story aloud, and everyone sits up a little straighter.
It is exciting to be chosen even if it means being criticized.
It is exciting to be criticized.

'What do we think?' he asks the class when he's finished.

'Well,' Sarah Pipp says, 'no offence, but the dialogue is kind of bad. Like, I get what the person is going for, but why doesn't the writer use contractions more?' Sarah Pipp reviews books for her blog, *The Paisley Unicorn Book Review*. She is always bragging about the free books she gets from publishers. 'And why third person? Why present tense? It makes the writing seem childish to me.'

Billy Lieberman, who writes about wronged boy heroes who overcome supernatural and parental obstacles, says. 'I don't even get what's supposed to have happened at the end? It's confusing.'

'I think it's ambiguous,' Mr Balboni says. 'Remember last week when we talked about ambiguity?'

Maggie Markakis, who is only in this elective because of a scheduling conflict involving maths and debate, says she likes it, though she notes discrepancies in the financial elements of the story.

Abner Shochet objects on multiple fronts: he doesn't like stories in which characters lie ('I am so done with unreliable narrators' – the concept had been introduced to them two weeks ago), and worse, he thinks nothing happens. This doesn't hurt Maya's feelings because all of Abner's stories end with the same twist: that everything had been a dream.

'Is there anything we liked about it?' Mr Balboni asks.

'The grammar,' Sarah Pipp says.

John Furness says, 'I liked how sad it was.' John has long brown eyelashes and a pop-idol pompadour. He wrote a story about his grandmother's hands that moved even hard-hearted Sarah Pipp to tears.

'Me too,' Mr Balboni says. 'As a reader, I responded to many of the things that you all objected to. I liked the somewhat formal style and the ambiguity. I disagree with the comment about the "unreliable narrators" – we may have to go over this concept again. I don't believe the financial elements were handled badly either. All things considered, I think this, along with John's story, "My Grandmother's Hands," are the two best stories from class this semester, and they will be the Alicetown High School entries to the county story contest.'

Abner groans. 'You didn't say who wrote the other one.'

'Right, of course. It's Maya. Round of applause for John and Maya.'

Maya tries not to look too pleased with herself.

'That's amazing, right? Mr Balboni picking us,' John says after class. He is following her to her locker, though Maya cannot say why.

'Yeah,' says Maya. 'I liked your story.' She *had* liked his story, but she really wants to win. First prize is a $150 Amazon gift voucher and a trophy.

'What would you buy if you won?' John asks.

'Not books. I have those from my dad.'

'You're lucky,' John says. 'I wish I lived in the bookstore.'

'I live above it, not in it, and it's not that great.'

'I bet it is.'

He sweeps his brown hair out of his eyes. 'My mom wants to know if you want to carpool to the ceremony.'

'But we just found out today,' Maya says.

'I know my mom. She always likes to carpool. Ask your dad.'

'The thing is, my dad will want to go, and he doesn't drive. So probably, Dad'll get my godmother or my god-father to drive us. And your mom will want to go, too. So I'm not sure if carpooling makes sense.' She feels like she's been talking for about a half hour.

He smiles at her, which makes his pompadour bounce a little. 'No problem. Maybe we could drive you somewhere else sometime?'

The award ceremony is held at a high school in Hyannis. Though it's just a gymnasium (the scent of balls of both varieties is still palpable) and the ceremony hasn't started yet, everyone speaks in hushed tones, like it's a church. Something important and literary is about to happen here.

Of the forty entries from the twenty high schools, only the top three stories will be read aloud. Maya has practised reading her story for John Furness. He recommended that she breathe more and slow down. She has been practising breathing and reading, which are not as easy to do as one might think. She had listened to him read, too. Her advice to him was to use his normal voice. He had been doing this faky, newscaster thing. 'You know you love it,' he had said. Now he talks to her in the fake voice all the time. It's so annoying.

Maya sees Mr Balboni talking to a person who can only be a teacher from another school. She is wearing teacher clothes – a floral dress and a beige cardigan with snow-flakes embroidered on it, and she is nodding adamantly at whatever Mr Balboni is saying. Of course, Mr Balboni is wearing his leather pants, and because he is out, a leather jacket – basically, a leather suit. Maya wants to take him to meet her father, because she wants A.J. to hear Mr Balboni praise her. The balance is that she doesn't want A.J. to be embarrassing. She had introduced A.J. to her English teacher, Mrs Smythe, at the store last month, and A.J. had pressed a book into the teacher's hands saying, 'You'll love this novel. It's exquisitely erotic.' Maya had wanted to die.

A.J. is wearing a tie, and Maya jeans. She had put on a dress that Amelia had chosen for her but decided that the dress made it seem like she cared too much. Amelia, who is in Providence this week, is meeting them there, but she'll probably run late. Maya knows she'll be sad about the dress.

A baton is tapped on the podium. The teacher in the snowflake sweater welcomes them to the Island County High School Short-Story Contest. She praises the entries for having been a particularly diverse and moving group. She says she loves her job and wishes everyone could win, and then she announces the first finalist.

Of course, John Furness would be a finalist. Maya sits back in her chair and listens. The story is better than she remembers. She likes the description of the grandmother's hands like tissue paper. She looks at A.J. to see how it is playing with him. He has a distant look in the eyes, which Maya recognizes as boredom.

The second story is by Virgina Kim from Blackheart High. 'The Journey' is about an adopted child from China.

A.J. nods a couple of times. She can tell he likes the story better than 'My Grandmother's Hands'.

Maya is starting to worry that she won't be picked at all. She is glad she wore jeans. She turns around to look for the quickest way out. Amelia is standing by the door of the auditorium. She gives Maya a thumbs-up sign. 'The dress. What happened to the dress?' Amelia mouths.

Maya shrugs, turns back to listen to 'The Journey'. Virginia Kim wears a black velvet dress with a white Peter Pan collar. She reads in a very soft voice, barely more than a whisper at times. It's as if she wants everyone to have to lean in to listen.

Unfortunately, 'The Journey' is endless, five times as long as 'My Grandmother's Hands', and after a while, Maya stops listening. Maya guesses it probably takes less time to fly to China.

If 'A Trip to the Beach' isn't in the top three, there will be T-shirts and cookies at the reception. But who wants to stay for the reception, if you don't at least place.

If she places, she won't be mad that she didn't win.

If John Furness wins, she will try not to hate him.

If Maya wins, maybe she will donate the gift voucher to charity. To, like, underprivileged kids or orphanages.

If she loses, it will be okay. She didn't write the story to win a prize or even complete an assignment. If she'd wanted to complete the assignment, she could have written about Puddleglum. Creative writing is graded pass/fail.

The third story is announced, and Maya grabs A.J.'s hand.

A Perfect Day for Bananafish

1948/J. D. Salinger

If something is good and universally acknowledged to be so, this is not reason enough to dislike it. (Side note: It has taken me all afternoon to write this sentence. My brain kept making a hash of the phrase 'universally acknowledged'.)

'A Trip to the Beach', your entry for the county short-story contest, reminds me a bit of Salinger's story. I mention this because I think you should have won first place. The first-place entry, which I believe was titled 'My Grandmother's Hands', was much simpler both formally, narratively, and certainly emotionally, than yours. Take heart, Maya. As a bookseller, I assure you that prize-winning can be somewhat important for sales but rarely matters much in terms of quality.

– A.J.F.

P.S. The thing I find most promising about your short story is that it shows empathy. Why do people do what they do? This is the hallmark of great writing.

P.P.S. If I have a criticism, perhaps it's that you might have introduced the swimming element earlier.

P.P.P.S. Also, readers will know what an ATM card is.

A TRIP TO THE BEACH

By Maya Tamerlane Fikry

Teacher: Edward Balboni, Alicetown High School

Grade 9

Mary is running late. She has a private room, but she shares the bathroom with six other people, and it seems like someone is always using it. When she gets back from the bathroom, the babysitter is sitting on her bed. 'Mary, I have been waiting for you for five minutes.'

'I'm sorry,' Mary says. 'I wanted to take a shower, but I couldn't get in.'

'It is already eleven,' the babysitter says. 'You've only paid me to be here until noon, and I have somewhere I need to be at 12:15 p.m. So you better not be late getting back.'

Mary thanks the babysitter. She kisses the baby on the head. 'Be good,' she says.

Mary runs across the campus to the English department. She runs up the stairs. Her teacher is already leaving by the time she gets there. 'Mary. I was just about to leave. I didn't think you were going to show. Please come in.'

Mary goes into the office. The teacher takes out

Mary's homework and sets it on the desk. 'Mary,' the teacher says. 'You used to get straight As, and now you are failing all of your classes.'

'I'm sorry,' Mary says. 'I'll try to do better.'

'Is something happening in your life?' the teacher asks. 'You used to be one of our best students.'

'No,' Mary says. She bites her lip.

'You have a scholarship to this college. You are already in trouble because your grades have been bad for a while, and when I tell the college, they will probably end your scholarship or at least make you leave for some time.'

'Please don't do that!' Mary begs. 'I don't have anywhere I can go. The only money I have is my scholarship money.'

'It is for your own good, Mary. You should go home and sort yourself out. Christmas is in a couple of weeks. Your parents will understand.'

Mary is fifteen minutes late getting back to the dorm. The babysitter is frowning when Mary gets there. 'Mary,' the babysitter says, 'you are late once again! When you're late, it makes me late for the things I have to do. I'm sorry. I really like the baby, but I don't think I can babysit for you any more.'

Mary takes the baby from the babysitter. 'Okay,' she says.

'Also,' the babysitter adds, 'you owe me for the last three times I babysat. It's ten dollars an hour so that's thirty dollars.'

'Can I pay you next time?' Mary asks. 'I meant to go to the automated teller machine (ATM) on my way back, but I didn't have time.'

The babysitter makes a face. 'Just put it in an envelope with my name on it and leave it at my dorm. I would really like the money before Christmas. I have presents to buy.'

Mary agrees.

'Bye, little baby,' the babysitter says. 'Have a great Christmas.'

The baby coos.

'Do you two have anything special planned for the holidays?' the babysitter asks.

'I'll probably take her to see my mom. She lives in Greenwich, Connecticut. She always has a big Christmas tree, and she makes a delicious dinner, and there will be tons of presents for me and for Myra.'

'That sounds really nice,' the babysitter says.

Mary puts the baby in the baby sling, and she walks to the bank. She checks the balance on her ATM card. She has $75.17 in her account. She takes out forty dollars and then she goes inside to get change.

She puts thirty dollars in an envelope with the babysitter's name on it. She buys a token for the subway and rides to the last stop on the train. The neighbourhood is not as nice as the neighbourhood where Mary's college is.

Mary walks down the street. She comes to a run-down

house with a chain-link fence out front. There is a dog tied to a post in the yard. It barks at the baby, and the baby starts to cry.

'Don't worry, baby,' Mary says. 'The dog can't get you.'

They go inside the house. The house is very dirty and there are kids everywhere. The kids are dirty, too. The kids are noisy and all different ages. Some of them are in wheelchairs or disabled.

'Hi, Mary,' a disabled girl says. 'What are you doing here?'

'I've come to see Mama,' Mary says.

'She is upstairs. She is not feeling well.'

'Thank you.'

'Mary, is that your baby?' the disabled girl asks.

'No,' Mary says. She bites her lip. 'I'm just watching it for a friend.'

'How is Harvard?' the disabled girl asks.

'Great,' Mary says.

'Bet you got all As.'

Mary shrugs.

'You are so modest, Mary. Still swimming in the swim team?'

Mary shrugs again. She walks up the stairs to see Mama.

Mama is a morbidly obese white woman. Mary is a skinny black girl. Mama cannot be Mary's biological mother.

'Hi, Mama,' Mary says. 'Merry Christmas.' Mary kisses the fat woman on the cheek.

'Hi, Mary. Miss Ivy Leaguer. Didn't expect to see you back here at your foster home.'

'No.'

'Is that your baby?' Mama asks.

Mary sighs. 'Yes.'

'What a shame,' Mama says. 'Smart girl like you, messing up her life. Didn't I tell you to never have sex? Didn't I tell you to always use protection?'

'Yes, Mama.' Mary bites her lip. 'Mama, would it be okay if the baby and I stayed here a while? I've decided to take some leave from the school to get my life organized. It would be very helpful.'

'Oh, Mary. I wish I could help, but the house is filled up. I don't have a room for you. You are too old for me to get a cheque from the state of Massachusetts.'

'Mama, I don't have anywhere else to go.'

'Mary, here is what I think you should do. I think you should contact the baby's father.'

Mary shakes her head. 'I didn't really know him that well.'

'Then I think you should put the baby up for adoption.'

Mary shakes her head again. 'I can't do that either.'

Mary goes back to the dorm room. She packs up a bag for the baby. She puts a stuffed Elmo in the bag. A girl from down the hall comes into Mary's room.

'Hey Mary, where are you going?'

Mary smiles brightly. 'I thought I would take a

trip to the beach,' she says. 'The baby loves the beach.'

'Isn't it a little cold for the beach?' the girl asks.

'Not really,' Mary says. 'The baby and I will wear our warmest clothes. Plus the beach is really nice in the winter.'

The girl shrugs. 'I guess.'

'When I was a little girl, my dad used to take me to the beach all the time.'

Mary drops off the envelope at the babysitter's dorm. At the train station, she uses her credit card to buy tickets for the train and boat that go to Alice Island.

'You do not need a ticket for the baby,' the ticket taker tells Mary.

'Good,' Mary says.

When she gets to Alice Island, the first place Mary sees is a bookstore. She goes inside so that she and the baby can warm up. A man is at the counter. He has a grumpy demeanour and he wears Converse sneakers.

Christmas music is playing in the store. The song is 'Have Yourself a Merry Little Christmas'.

'This song makes me so sad,' a customer says. 'This is the saddest song I have ever heard. Why would anyone write such a sad Christmas song?'

'I'm looking for something to read,' Mary says.

The man gets slightly less grumpy. 'What kind of books do you like?'

'Oh, all kinds, but my favourite kind of book is

the kind where a character has hardships but over-
comes them in the end. I know life isn't like that.
Maybe that is why it is my favourite thing.'

The bookseller says that he has the perfect thing
for her, but by the time he gets back, Mary is gone.
'Miss?'

He leaves the book on the counter just in case Mary
decides to come back.

Mary is on the beach, but the baby is not with her.

She used to swim in a swim team. She was good
enough to win the state championships in high school.
That day, the waves are choppy and the water is cold,
and Mary is out of practice.

She swims out, past the lighthouse, and she doesn't
swim back.

                            THE END

'Congratulations,' Maya tells John Furness at the reception.
She is clutching her rolled-up T-shirt in her hand. Amelia
has Maya's certificate: third place.

John shrugs and his hair flops back and forth. 'I thought
you should have won, but it's pretty cool them picking two
stories from Alicetown as finalists.'

'Maybe Mr Balboni is a good teacher.'

'We can split my gift certificate if you want,' John says.
Maya shakes her head. She doesn't want it that way.

'What would you have bought?'

'I was going to give it to charity. To underprivileged
kids.'

'Seriously?' He does his newscaster voice.

'My dad doesn't really like us to shop online.'

'You aren't angry at me, are you?' John says.

'No. I'm happy for you. Go whales!' She punches him on the shoulder.

'Ow.'

'I'll see you around. We've got to catch the auto ferry back to Alice.'

'So do we,' John says. 'There's plenty of time for us to hang out.'

'My dad has things to do at the store.'

'See you at school,' John says in the newscaster voice again.

In the car on the way home, Amelia congratulates Maya for placing and for writing an amazing story, and A.J. says nothing.

Maya thinks that A.J. must be disappointed in her, but just before they get out of the car, he says, 'These things are never fair. People like what they like, and that's the great and terrible thing. It's about personal taste and a certain set of people on a certain day. For instance, two out of the three finalists were women, which might have tipped the scales toward the male. Or maybe one of the judges' grandmothers died last week, which made that story particularly effective. One never knows. But here is what I do know. "A Trip to the Beach" by Maya Tamerlane Fikry was written by a writer.' She thinks he's about to hug her, but instead he shakes her hand, the way he would greet a colleague – perhaps an author visiting the store.

A sentence occurs to her: *The day my father shook my hand, I knew I was a writer.*

Just before the school year ends, A.J. and Amelia make an offer on a house. The house is about ten minutes away from the store and inland. Although it does have four bedrooms, two bathrooms, and the quiet that A.J. believes a young writer needs to work, the house is no one's idea of a dream house. The last owner had died there – she hadn't wanted to leave, but she hadn't done much to maintain the house in the last fifty or so years either. The ceilings are low; there are several different eras of wallpaper to be stripped; the foundation is shaky. A.J. calls it the 'in-ten-years house' meaning that 'in ten years, it might be livable'. Amelia calls it 'a project' and she sets herself to working on it immediately. Maya, having recently made her way through the *Lord of the Rings* trilogy, names it Bag End. 'Because it looks as if a hobbit might live here.'

A.J. kisses his daughter on the forehead. He is delighted to have produced such a fantastic nerd.

The Tell-Tale Heart

1843/E. A. Poe

True!

Maya, perhaps you don't know that I had a wife before Amelia and a profession before I became a bookseller. I was once married to a woman named Nicole Evans. I loved her very much. She died in a car accident, and a large part of me was dead for a long time after, probably until I found you.

Nicole and I met in college and married the summer before we entered graduate school. She wanted to be a poet but in the meantime was unhappily working toward a PhD in twentieth-century female poets (Adrienne Rich, Marianne Moore, Elizabeth Bishop; how she hated Sylvia Plath.) I was well on my way to a PhD in American literature. My dissertation was to be on depictions of disease in the works of E. A. Poe, a subject I had never particularly liked but had grown to truly despise. Nic suggested that there could be better, happier ways to have a literary life. I said, 'Yeah, like what?'

And she said, 'Bookstore owners.'

'Tell me more,' I said.

'Did you know my hometown doesn't have a bookstore?'

'Really? Alice seems like the kind of place that should have one.'

'I know,' she said. 'A place is not truly a place without a bookstore.'

And so we quit grad school, took her trust fund money, moved to Alice, and opened the store that would become Island Books.

Does it go without saying that we did not know what we were getting into?

In the years after Nicole's accident, I often imagined what my life might have been like if I had finished that PhD.

But I digress.

This is arguably the best known of E. A. Poe's stories. In a box marked 'ephemera', you'll find my notes and twenty-five pages of my dissertation (most of it concerning 'The Tell-Tale Heart'), if you're ever interested in reading more about the things your dad did in another life.

— A.J.F.

'What bothers me in a story more than anything is a loose end,' Deputy Doug Lippman says, selecting four mini-quiches from the hors d'oeuvres Lambiase has provided. After many years of hosting the Chief's Choice Book Club, Lambiase knows that the most important thing, even more than the title at hand, is food and drink.

'Deputy,' Lambiase says, 'it's a three-quiche max, or there won't be enough for everyone.'

The deputy puts a quiche back on the tray. 'Like, okay, what the heck happened to the violin? Did I miss something? A priceless Stradivarius doesn't vanish into thin air.'

'Good point,' Lambiase says. 'Anyone?'

'You know what I freaking hate,' Kathy from Homicide says. 'I freaking hate shoddy police work. Like, when no one wears gloves, I'm yelling, *Shut up, you're contaminating the crime scene!*'

'You never get that in Deaver,' Sylvio from Dispatch says.

'If only they could all be Deaver,' Lambiase says.

'But what I hate more than bad police work is when everything is solved too quickly,' Homicide Kathy continues. 'Even Deaver does it. Things take time to figure out. Sometimes years. You got to live with a case a long time.'

'Good point, Kathy.'

'These mini-quiches are delicious, by the way.'

'Costco,' Lambiase says.

'I hate the women characters,' Rosie the firefighter says. 'The policewomen are always ex-models from families of cops. She's got, like, one flaw.'

'Bites her nails,' says Homicide Kathy. 'Unruly hair. Big mouth.'

Rosie the firefighter laughs. 'It's some fantasy of a lady in law enforcement is what it is.'

'I dunno,' Deputy Dave says. 'I like the fantasy.'

'Maybe the writer's point is that the violin is not the point?' Lambiase says.

'Of course it's the point,' says Deputy Dave.

'Maybe the point is how the violin affects everyone's lives?' Lambiase continues.

'Boo,' Rosie the firefighter says. She makes a thumbs-down sign. 'Booooo.'

From the counter, A.J. listens to the discussion. Of the dozen or so book groups Island hosts, Chief's Choice is his favourite by far. Lambiase calls over to him, 'Back me up here, A.J. You don't always have to know who stole the violin.'

'In my experience, a book is more satisfying to readers if you do,' A.J. says. 'Although I don't mind ambiguity myself.'

The group's cheers drown out everything after the word *do*.

'Traitor!' Lambiase yells.

At that moment, the wind chimes sound and Ismay enters the store. The group goes back to discussing the book, but Lambiase can't help staring at her. She has a white summer dress on with a full skirt that emphasizes her tiny waist. She wears her red hair long again, which softens her face. He is reminded of the orchids that his ex-wife used to keep in the front window.

Ismay goes up to A.J. She sets a piece of paper on the counter. 'I've finally picked the play,' she says. 'I'll probably need about fifty copies of *Our Town*.'

'It's a classic,' A.J. says.

Many years after Daniel Parish's death and a half hour after Chief's Choice, Lambiase decides enough time has passed to make a particular inquiry of A.J. 'I hate to overstep here, but would you check if your sister-in-law is interested in going on a date with a not-bad-looking law enforcement officer?'

'To whom are you referring?'

'Me. I was kidding about the not-bad-looking part. I know I'm not exactly the blue-ribbon cow.'

'No, I meant who do you want me to ask? Amelia is an only child.'

'Not Amelia. I mean, your ex-sister-in-law, Ismay.'

'Oh, right. Ismay.' A.J. pauses. '*Ismay? Really? Her?*'

'Yeah, I've always kind of had a thing for her. Going way back to high school. Not that she ever noticed me very much. I figure none of us is getting any younger, so I should take my chances now.'

A.J. calls Ismay on the phone and makes the request.

'Lambiase?' she asks. '*Him?*'

'He's a good guy,' A.J. says.

'It's only ... well, I've never dated a police officer before,' Ismay says.

'That's starting to sound awfully snobbish.'

'I don't mean to sound that way, but blue-collar men have never been my type.'

And that worked out so well with you and Daniel, A.J. thinks but does not say.

'Of course, my marriage *was* a disaster,' Ismay says.

Several evenings later, she and Lambiase are at El Corazon. She orders the surf and turf, and a gin and tonic. No need to put on a show of femininity as she suspects there won't be a second date.

'Good appetite,' Lambiase comments. 'I'll have the same.'

'So,' Ismay says, 'what do you do when you aren't being a cop?'

'Well, believe it or not,' he says shyly, 'I read a lot. Maybe you wouldn't think it's that much. I know you teach English.'

'What do you read?' Ismay asks.

'Little bit of everything. I started with crime novels. Pretty predictable that, I guess. But then A.J. got me into other kinds of books, too. Literary fiction, I think you'd call it. Some of it doesn't have enough action for my taste. Kind of embarrassing, but I like young adult. Plenty of action there and feelings, too. I also read whatever A.J.'s reading. He's partial to short stories—'

'I know.'

'And whatever Maya's reading, too. I like talking about books with them. They're book people, you know. I also host a book group for the other cops. Maybe you've seen the signs for the Chief's Choice?'

Ismay shakes her head.

'Sorry if I'm talking too much. I'm nervous, I guess.'

'You're fine.' Ismay sips her drink. 'Did you ever read any of Daniel's books?'

'Yeah, one. The first one.'

'Did you like it?'

'Not my cup of tea. It was very well written, though.' Ismay nods.

'Do you miss your husband?' Lambiase asks.

'Not really,' she says after a bit. 'His sense of humour sometimes. But the best parts of him were in his books. I suppose I could always read those if I missed him too much. I haven't wanted to read one yet, though.' Ismay laughs a little.

'What do you read, then?'

'Plays, the odd bit of poetry. Then there are the books I teach every year: *Tess of the d'Urbervilles*, *Johnny Got His Gun*, *A Farewell to Arms*, *A Prayer for Owen Meany*, some years *Wuthering Heights*, *Silas Marner*, *Their Eyes Were Watching God* or *I Capture the Castle*. Those books are like old friends.

'When I'm choosing something new, though, something just for myself, my favourite kind of character is a woman in a faraway place. India. Or Bangkok. Sometimes she leaves her husband. Sometimes she never had a husband because she knew, wisely, that married life would not be for her. I like when she has multiple lovers. I like when she wears hats to block her fair skin from the sun. I like when she travels and has adventures. I like descriptions of hotels and suitcases with stickers on them. I like descriptions of food and clothes and jewellery. A little romance but not too much. The story is period. No cellphones. No social networking. No Internet at all. Ideally, it's set in the 1920s or the 1940s. Maybe there's a war going on, but it's just a backdrop. No bloodshed. Some sex but nothing too graphic. No children. Children often spoil a story for me.'

'I don't have any,' Lambiase says.

'I don't mind them in real life. I just don't want to read about them. Endings can be happy or sad, I don't care any more as long as it's earned. She can settle down, maybe open a little business, or she can drown herself in the ocean. Finally, a nice-looking jacket is important. I don't care how good the insides are. I don't want to spend any length of time with an ugly object. I'm shallow, I guess.'

'You are one heck of a pretty woman,' Lambiase says.

'I'm ordinary,' she says.

'No way.'

'Pretty is not a good reason to court someone, you know. I have to tell that to my students all the time.'

'This from the woman who doesn't read the books with the ugly covers.'

'Well, I'm warning you. I could be a bad book with a good jacket.'

He groans. 'I've known a few of those.'

'For instance?'

'My first marriage. The wife was pretty but mean.'

'So you thought you'd make the same mistake twice?'

'Nah, I've seen you on the shelf for years. I've read the synopsis and the quotes on the back. Caring teacher. God-mother. Upstanding community member. Caretaker to sister's husband and daughter. Bad marriage, probably made too young, but tried her best.'

'Sketchy,' she says.

'But it's enough to make me want to read on.' He smiles at her. 'Should we order dessert?'

'I haven't had sex in a really long time,' Ismay says in the car on the way back to her house.

'Okay,' Lambiase says.

'I think we should have sex,' Ismay clarifies. 'If you want to, I mean.'

'I do want to,' Lambiase says. 'But not if that means I don't get to take you on a second date. I don't want to be a warm-up for the guy that gets you.'

She laughs at him and leads him to her bedroom. She takes off her clothes with the lights on. She wants him to see what a fifty-one-year-old woman looks like.

Lambiase lets out a low whistle.

'You're sweet, but you should have seen me before,' she says. 'Surely you see the scars.'

A long one runs from her knee to her hip. Lambiase runs his thumb along it: it's like a seam on a doll. 'Yeah, I see them, but it doesn't take away from anything.'

Her leg had been broken in fifteen places and she'd had to have the socket of her right hip replaced, but other than that, she'd been fine. For once in his life, Daniel had taken the brunt of the impact.

'Does it hurt much?' Lambiase asks. 'Should I be careful?'

She shakes her head and tells him to take off his clothes.

*

In the morning, she wakes before him. 'I'm going to make you breakfast,' she says. He nods sleepily, and then she kisses him on his shaven head.

'Are you shaving this because you're balding or because you like the style?' she asks.

'A little of both,' Lambiase replies.

She sets a towel on the bed, then leaves the room. Lambiase takes his time getting ready. He opens the drawer of her nightstand and pokes around her things a bit. She has expensive-looking lotions that smell like her. He smears some on his hands. He opens her closet. Her clothes are tiny. There are silk dresses, pressed cotton blouses, wool pencil skirts and paper-thin cashmere cardigans. Everything is in smart shades of beige and grey, and the condition of her clothes is immaculate. He looks at the top shelf of the closet, where her shoes are neatly organized in their original boxes. Above one of the stacks of shoes, he notices a small child's backpack in princess pink.

His cop eyes clock the child's backpack as out of place somehow. He knows he shouldn't, but he pulls it down and unzips it. Inside is a zipper case with crayons and a couple of colouring books. He picks up a colouring book. MAYA is written across the front. Behind the colouring book is another book. A flimsy thing, more like a pamphlet than a book. Lambiase looks at the cover:

TAMERLANE

AND

OTHER POEMS.

BY A BOSTONIAN.

Crayon marks scar the cover.

Lambiase doesn't know what to make of it.

His cop brain clicks in, formulating the following ques-
tions: (1) Is this A.J.'s stolen *Tamerlane*? (2) Why would
Tamerlane be in Ismay's possession? (3) How did *Tamerlane* get
covered in crayon and who did the colouring? Maya? (4)
Why would *Tamerlane* be in a backpack with Maya's name
in it?

He is about to run downstairs to demand an explanation
from Ismay, but then he changes his mind.

He looks at the ancient manuscript for several seconds
longer.

He can smell the pancakes from where he sits. He can
imagine her downstairs making them. She is probably
wearing a white apron and a silky nightgown. Or maybe
she is wearing the apron and nothing else. That would be
exciting. Maybe they can have sex again. Not on the
kitchen table. It is not comfortable to have sex on a kitchen
table no matter how erotic it looks in movies. Maybe on the
couch. Maybe back upstairs. Her mattress is so soft, and
her sheets' thread count must be in the thousands.

Lambiase prides himself on being a good cop, and he
knows he should go downstairs and make an excuse to her
now about why he has to go.

But is that the sound of an orange being juiced? Is she
warming syrup, too?

The book is ruined.

Besides which, it was stolen so long ago. Over ten years
now. A.J. is happily married. Maya is settled. Ismay has suffered.

Not to mention, he really likes this woman. And none of this is Lambiase's business anyway. He zips the book back into the backpack and puts the bag back where he found it.

Lambiase believes that cops go one of two ways as they get older. They either get more judgmental or less so. Lambiase is not so rigid as when he was a young police officer. He has found that people do all sorts of things, and they usually have their reasons.

He goes downstairs and sits at her kitchen table, which is round and covered with the whitest tablecloth he has ever seen. 'Smells great,' he says.

'Nice to have someone to cook for. You were up there a long time,' she says, pouring him a glass of fresh-squeezed orange juice. Her apron is turquoise, and she is wearing black exercise clothes.

'Hey,' Lambiase says, 'did you happen to read Maya's short story for the contest? I thought the kid should have been a shoo-in to win.'

'I haven't read it yet,' Ismay says.

'It's basically Maya's version of the last day of her mother's life,' Lambiase says.

'She's so precocious,' Ismay says.

'I've always wondered why Maya's mother chose Alice.'

Ismay flips a pancake, and then she flips another. 'Who knows why people do what they do?'

Ironhead

2005/Aimee Bender

For the record, everything new is not worse than everything old.

Parents with heads made from pumpkins have a baby with a head made from iron. I have, for what I assume will be very obvious reasons, been thinking about this one a lot lately.

— A.J.F.

P.S. I also find myself thinking of 'Bullet in the Brain' by Tobias Wolff. You might give that a read, too.

Christmas brings A.J.'s mother, who looks nothing like him. Paula is a tiny white woman with long grey hair that has not been cut since she retired from her job at a computer company a decade ago. She has made the most of her retirement in Arizona. She makes jewellery out of rocks that she paints. She teaches literacy to inmates. She rescues Siberian huskies. She tries to go to a different restaurant every week. She dates some – women and men. She has slipped into bisexuality without needing to make a big thing about it. She is seventy, and she believes you try new things or you may as well die. She comes bearing three identically wrapped and shaped presents for the family and a promise that it isn't thoughtlessness that has led her to pick the same gift for the three of them. 'It's something I thought the whole family would appreciate and use,' she says.

Maya knows what it is before she's even through the paper.

She's seen them at school. Almost everyone seems to have one these days, but her dad doesn't approve. She slows down her unwrapping speed to allow herself time to figure out the response that will least offend both her grandmother and her father.

'An e-reader! I've wanted one for a really long time.' She shoots a quick look over to her father. He nods, though his eyebrow is twitching slightly. 'Thanks, Nana.' Maya kisses her grandmother on the cheek.

'Thank you, Mother Fikry,' says Amelia. She already has an e-reader for work, but she keeps this information to herself.

As soon as he sees what it is, A.J. decides to stop unwrapping the present. If he keeps it in the paper, perhaps it can be given to someone else. 'Thank you, Mother,' A.J. says, and then he bites his tongue.

'A.J., you have a moue,' his mother notes.

'I don't,' he insists.

'You must keep up with the times,' she continues.

'Why must I? What is so great about the times?' A.J. has often reflected that, bit by bit, all the best things in the world are being carved away like fat from meat. First, it had been the record stores, and then the video stores, and then newspapers and magazines, and now even the big chain bookstores were disappearing everywhere you looked. From his point of view, the only thing worse than a world with big chain bookstores was a world with NO big chain bookstores. At least the big stores sell books and not pharmaceuticals or lumber! At least some of the people who work at those stores have degrees in English literature and know how to read and curate books for people! At least the big stores can sell ten thousand units of publishers' dreck so that Island gets to sell one hundred units of literary fiction!

'The easiest way to get old is to be technologically behind, A.J.' After twenty-five years in computers, his mother had come away with a respectable pension and this one opinion, A.J. thinks uncharitably.

A.J. takes a deep breath, a long drink of water, another deep breath. His brain feels tight against his skull. His mother visits rarely, and he doesn't want to spoil their time together.

'Dad, you're turning a bit red,' Maya says.

'A.J., are you unwell?' his mother asks.

He puts his fist down on the coffee table. 'Mother, do you even understand that that infernal device is not only going to single-handedly destroy my business but, worse than that, send centuries of a vibrant literary culture into what will surely be an unceremonious and rapid decline?' A.J. asks.

'You're being dramatic,' Amelia says. 'Calm down.'

'Why should I calm down? I do not like the present. I do not like that thing and certainly not three of that thing in my house. I would rather you have bought my daughter something less destructive like a crack pipe.'

Maya giggles.

A.J.'s mother looks like she might cry. 'Well, I certainly didn't want to make anyone upset.'

'It's fine,' Amelia says. 'It's a lovely gift. We all love to read, and I'm sure we'll enjoy using them very much. Besides, A.J. really is being dramatic.'

'I'm sorry, A.J.,' his mother says. 'I didn't know you'd have such strong feelings about the matter.'

'You could have asked!'

'Shut up, A.J. Stop apologizing, Mother Fikry,' Amelia says. 'It's the *perfect* gift for a family of readers. Lots of bookstores are figuring out ways to sell e-books along with conventional paper books. A.J. just doesn't want to—'

A.J. interrupts. 'You know that's bullshit, Amy!'

'You are being so rude,' Amelia says. 'You can't put your head in the sand and act like e-readers don't exist. That's no way to deal with anything.'

'Do you smell smoke?' Maya asks.

A second later, the fire alarm goes off.

'Oh hell!' Amelia says. 'The brisket!' She runs into the kitchen, and A.J. follows her. 'I had my phone set to go off, but it didn't.'

'I put your phone on silent so that it wouldn't *ruin Christmas*!' A.J. says.

'You what? Stop touching my phone.'

'Why not use the timer that came with the oven?'

'Because I DO NOT TRUST IT! That oven is about one hundred years old like everything else in this house if you haven't noticed!' Amelia yells as she removes the flaming brisket from the oven.

As the brisket is ruined, Christmas dinner consists entirely of side dishes.

'I like the sides the best,' A.J.'s mother says.

'Me too,' Maya says.

'No substance,' A.J. mutters. 'They leave you hungry.' He has a headache, which he does no favours by drinking several glasses of red wine.

'Would someone ask A.J. to pass the wine?' Amelia says. 'And would someone tell A.J. he is hogging the bottle?'

'Very mature,' A.J. says. He pours her another glass.

'I honestly can't wait to try it out, Nana,' Maya whispers to her stricken grandmother. 'I'm going to wait until I go to bed.' She darts her eyes toward A.J. '*You know.*'

'I think that's a very good idea,' A.J.'s mother whispers back.

That night in bed, A.J. is still talking about the e-reader. 'Do you know the real problem with that contraption?'

'I suppose you are about to tell me,' Amelia says without looking up from her paper book.

'Everyone thinks they have good taste, but most people do not have good taste. In fact, I'd argue that most people have terrible taste. When left to their own devices – literally their own devices – they read crap and they don't know the difference.'

'Do you know what the good thing about e-readers is?' Amelia asks.

'No, Madame Bright Side,' A.J. says. 'And I don't want to.'

'Well, for those of us with husbands who are growing far-sighted, and I'm not going to mention any names here. For those of us with husbands who are rapidly becoming middle-aged and losing their vision. For those of us burdened by pathetic half men for spouses—'

'Get to it, Amy!'

'An e-reader allows these cursed creatures to enlarge the text as much as they'd like.'

A.J. says nothing.

Amelia sets down her book to smile smugly at her husband, but when she looks over the man is frozen. A.J. is having one of his episodes. The episodes trouble Amelia, though she reminds herself not to be worried.

A minute and a half later, A.J. comes to. 'I've always been a bit far-sighted,' he says. 'It's not about being middle-aged.'

She wipes the spittle from the corners of his mouth with a Kleenex.

'Christ, did I just black out?' A.J. asks.

'You did.'

He grabs the tissue from Amelia. He is not the type of man who likes being tended to in this way. 'How long?'

'About ninety seconds, I'd guess.' Amelia pauses. 'Is that long or average?'

'Maybe a bit long but basically average.'

'Do you think you should go in for a check-up?'

'No,' A.J. says. 'You know I've had these since I was a chive.'

'A chive?' she asks.

'A child. What did I say?' A.J. gets out of bed and heads to the bathroom, and Amelia follows him. 'Please, Amy. A little space.'

'I don't want to give you space,' she says.

'Fine.'

'I want you to go to the doctor. That's three of these since Thanksgiving.'

A.J. shakes his head. 'My health insurance is crap, Amy darling. And Dr Rosen will say it's the same thing I've had for years anyway. I'll go see the doctor in March for my annual like I always do.'

Amelia goes into the bathroom. 'Maybe Dr Rosen can give you a new medication?' She squeezes between him and the bathroom mirror, resting her generous bum on the new double-sink counter that they installed last month. 'You are very important, A.J.'

'I'm not exactly the president,' he retorts.

'You are the father of Maya. And the love of my life. And a purveyor of culture to this community.'

A.J. rolls his eyes, then he kisses Amelia the bright-sider on the mouth.

Christmas and New Year's are over; his mother is happily returned to Arizona; Maya is back at school and Amelia at work. The real gift of the holiday season, A.J. thinks, is that it ends. He likes the routine. He likes making breakfast in the morning. He likes running to work.

He puts on his running clothes, does a few half-hearted stretches, throws a headband over his ears, straps on his backpack, and prepares to run to the store. Now that he no longer lives above the store, his route takes him in the opposite direction to the one he used to take when Nic was alive, when Maya was a baby, in the first years of his marriage to Amelia.

He runs past Ismay's house, which she once shared with Daniel and now shares improbably with Lambiase. He runs past the spot where Daniel died, too. He runs past the old dance studio. What was the dance teacher's name? He knows she moved to California not too long ago, and the dance studio is empty. He wonders who will teach the little girls of Alice Island to dance? He runs past Maya's elementary school and past her junior high and past her high school. *High school.* She has a boyfriend. The Furness boy is a writer. He hears them arguing all the time. He takes a short cut through a field, and is almost through it to Captain Wiggins Street when he blacks out.

It is twenty-two degrees out, and when he wakes his hand is blue from where it had rested on the ice.

He stands and warms his hands on his jacket. He has never passed out in the middle of a run before.

'Madame Olenska,' he says.

Dr Rosen gives him a full examination. A.J. is in good health for his age, but there's something strange about his eyes that gives the doctor pause.

'Have you had any other problems?' she asks.

'Well . . . Perhaps it's just growing older, but lately I seem to have a verbal glitch every now and again.'

'Glitch?' she says.

'I catch myself. It's not that bad. But I occasionally switch a word with another word. *Child* for *chive*, for example. Or last week I called *The Grapes of Wrath* *The Grapefruit Rag*. Obviously, this poses a problem in my line of work. I felt quite convinced that I was saying the right thing. My wife thought there might be an anti-seizure medication that could help?'

'Aphasia,' she says. 'I don't like the sound of that.' Given A.J.'s history of seizures, the doctor decides to send him to a brain specialist in Boston.

'How's Molly doing?' A.J. asks by way of changing the subject. The surly salesgirl hasn't worked for him for six or seven years now.

'She's just been accepted to . . . ' And the doctor names a writing programme, but A.J. isn't paying attention. He is thinking about his brain. It strikes him that it is odd to have to use the thing that may not be working to consider the thing that isn't working. ' . . . thinks she's going to write the Great American Novel. I suppose I have you and Nicole to blame,' the doctor says.

'Full responsibility,' A.J. says.

Glioblastoma multiforme.

'Would you mind spelling that for me?' A.J. asks. He has not brought anyone to this appointment with him. He has not wanted anyone to know until he was certain. 'I'd like to Google it later.'

The cancer is so rare that the oncologist at Massachusetts General Hospital has never seen a case other than in a scholarly publication and once on the television show *Grey's Anatomy*.

'What happened to the case in the publication?' A.J. asks.

'Death. Two years,' the oncologist says.

'Two good years?'

'One pretty good year, I'd say.'

A.J. goes for the second opinion. 'And on the TV show?'

The oncologist laughs, a noisy chainsaw of a laugh designed to be the loudest sound in the room. See, cancer is hilarious. 'I don't think we should be making prognoses based on nighttime soap operas, Mr Fikry.'

'What happened?'

'I believe the patient had the surgery, lived for an episode or two, thought he was in the clear, proposed to his doctor girlfriend, had a heart attack that was, apparently, unrelated to the brain cancer, and died the next episode.'

'Oh.'

'My sister writes for television, and I believe television writers call this a three-episode arc.'

'So I should expect to live somewhere between three episodes and two years.'

The oncologist chainsaw-laughs again. 'Good. A sense of humour is key. I should say that estimate sounds about right.' The oncologist wants to schedule surgery immediately.

'Immediately?'

'Your symptoms were masked by your seizure, Mr Fikry. And the scans show that this tumour is quite far advanced. I wouldn't wait if I were you.'

The surgery will cost nearly as much as the down payment on their house. It is unclear how much A.J.'s meagre small-businessperson insurance will cover. 'If I have the surgery, how much time does it buy me?' A.J. asks.

'Depends on how much we're able to get out. Ten years, if we manage clean margins. Two years, maybe, if not. The kind of tumour you have has the annoying tendency to grow back.'

'And if you're successful removing the thing, am I left a vegetable?'

'We don't like to use terms like *vegetable*, Mr Fikry. But it's in your left frontal lobe. You'll likely experience the occasional verbal deficit. Increased aphasia, et cetera. But we won't take out so much that you aren't left mostly yourself. Of course, if left untreated, the tumour will grow until the language centre of your brain is pretty much gone. Whether we treat or not, this will, in all likelihood, happen eventually anyway.'

Weirdly, A.J. thinks of Proust. Though he pretends to have read the whole thing, A.J. has only ever read the first volume of *In Search of Lost Time*. It had been a struggle to read that much, and now what he thinks is, *At least I will never have to read the rest.* 'I have to discuss this with my wife and my daughter,' he says.

'Yes, of course,' the oncologist says, 'but don't delay too long.'

On the train then the ferry back to Alice, he thinks about Maya's college and Amelia's ability to pay the mortgage on the house they bought less than a year ago. By the time he is walking down Captain Wiggins Street, he decides that he cannot undertake such a surgery if it means leaving his nearest and dearest broke.

A.J. does not yet want to face his family at home so he calls Lambiase, and the two of them meet at the bar.

'Tell me a good cop story,' A.J. says.

'Like a story about a good cop or a story that is interesting involving police officers?'

'Either one. It's up to you. I want to hear something amusing that will distract me from my problems.'

'What problems do you have? Perfect wife. Perfect kid. Good business.'

'I'll tell you after.'

Lambiase nods. 'Okay. Let me think. Maybe fifteen years ago, there was this kid, goes to Alicetown. He hasn't been to school for a month. Every day, he tells his parents he'll go, and every day, he doesn't show up. Even if they leave him there, he sneaks out and goes somewhere else.'

'Where's he going?'

'Right. The parents think he must be in some serious trouble. He's a tough kid, hangs with a tough crowd. They all get bad grades and wear low pants. His parents run a food stand at the beach, so there isn't much money. Anyhow, the parents are at their wits' end, so I decide to follow the kid the whole day. The kid goes to school, and then between period one and two, he just leaves. I'm trailing behind him, and finally we get to a building I've never been into before. I'm on Main and Parker. You know where I am?'

'That's the library.'

'Bingo. You know I never read much back then. So I follow him up the stairs and into a library carrel in the back and I'm thinking, he's probably going to do drugs or something there. Perfect place, right? Isolated. But you know what he's got?'

'Books, I'd imagine. That's the obvious thing, right?'

'He's got one thick book. He's in the middle of *Infinite Jest*. You ever heard of it?'

'Now you're making this up.'

'The boy is reading *Infinite Jest*. He says he can't do it at home because he has five siblings to babysit and he can't do it at school because his buddies will make fun of him. So he skips school to go read in peace. The book takes a lot of concentration. "Listen, *hombre*," he says, "there's nothing for me at school. Everything's in this book."'

'I take it he's Latino, by your use of the word *hombre*. A lot of Hispanic people on Alice Island?'

'A few.'

'So what do you do?'

'I haul his ass back to school. The principal asks me how the kid should be punished. I ask the kid how long he thinks it'll take him to finish the book. He says, "About two weeks." And so I recommend they give him a two-week suspension for delinquency.'

'You're definitely making this up,' A.J. says. 'Admit it. The troubled youth was not skipping school to read *Infinite Jest.*'

'He was, A.J. I swear to God.' But then Lambiase bursts out laughing. 'You seemed depressed. I wanted to tell you a story with a little uplift.'

'Thanks. Thanks very much.'

A.J. orders another beer.

'What did you want to tell me?'

'It's funny that you should mention *Infinite Jest.* Why did you choose that particular title, by the way?' A.J. says.

'I always see it in the store. It takes up a lot of space on the shelf.'

A.J. nods. 'I once had this huge argument with a friend of mine about it. He loved it. I hated it. But the funniest thing about this dispute, the thing I will confess to you now is—'

'Yes?'

'That I never finished reading it.' A.J. laughs. 'That and Proust can both go on my list of unfinished works, thank God. My brain is broken, by the way.' He takes out the slip of paper and reads, 'Glioblastoma multiforme. It turns you into a vegetable and then you die. But at least it's quick.'

Lambiase sets down his beer. 'There must be a surgery or something,' he says.

'There is, but it costs a billion dollars. And it only delays things anyway. I won't leave Amy and Maya broke just to prolong my life by a couple of months.'

Lambiase finishes his beer. He signals the bartender for another one. 'I think you should let them decide for themselves,' Lambiase says.

'They'll be sentimental,' A.J. says.

'Let them be.'

'The right thing for me to do is blow my stupid brains out, I'd say.'

Lambiase shakes his head. 'You'd do that to Maya?'

'How is it better for her to have a brain-dead father and no money for college?'

That night in bed, after the lights are off, Lambiase pulls Ismay close to him. 'I love you,' he tells her. 'And I want you to know that I don't judge you for anything you might have done in the past.'

'Okay,' Ismay says. 'I'm half asleep and I don't know what you're talking about.'

'I know about the bag in the closet,' Lambiase whispers. 'I know that the book's in there. I don't know how it got there and I don't need to know either. But it's only right that it be returned to its rightful owner.'

After a long pause, Ismay says. 'The book's ruined.'

'But even a damaged *Tamerlane* might still be worth something,' Lambiase says. 'I searched the Christie's website and the last copy on the market sold for five hundred sixty thousand dollars. So I figure maybe a damaged one is worth fifty thousand or something. And A.J. and Amy need the money.'

'Why do they need the money?'

He tells her about A.J.'s cancer, and Ismay covers her face with her hands.

'The way I see it,' Lambiase says, 'we wipe the book down of fingerprints, put it in an envelope, and return it. No one has to know where or who it came from.'

Ismay turns on the bedside lamp. 'How long have you known about this?'

'Since the first night I spent at your house.'

'And you didn't care? Why didn't you turn me in?' Ismay's eyes are sharp.

'Because it wasn't my business, Izzie. I wasn't invited in your home as an officer of the law. And I didn't have a right to be looking through your stuff. And I figured there must be a story. You're a good woman, Ismay, and you haven't had it easy.'

Ismay sits up. Her hands are shaking. She walks over to the closet and pulls down the bag. 'I want you to know what happened,' she says.

'I don't need to,' Lambiase says.

'Please, I want to tell you. And don't interrupt. If you interrupt me, I won't be able to get it all out.'

'Okay, Izzie,' he says.

'The first time Marian Wallace came to see me, I was five months pregnant. She had Maya with her, and the baby was about two. Marian Wallace was very young, very pretty, very tall with tired, golden-brown eyes. She

said, "Maya is Daniel's daughter." And I said – and I'm
not proud of this – "How do I know you aren't lying?"
I could see perfectly well that she wasn't lying. I knew my
husband after all. I knew his type. He had cheated on
me from the day we were married and probably before
that, too. But I loved his books or at least that first one.
And I felt like somewhere down deep inside him the
person who wrote it must be there. That you couldn't
write such beautiful things and have such an ugly heart.
But that is the truth. He was a beautiful writer and a
terrible person.

'I can't blame Daniel for all of this, though. I can't blame
him for my part in it. I screamed at Marian Wallace. She
was twenty-two, but she looked like a kid. "Do you think
you're the first slut to show up here, claiming to have had
Daniel's baby?"

'She apologized, kept apologizing. She said, "The baby
doesn't have to be in Daniel Parish's life" – she kept calling
him by his first and last name. She was a fan, you see. She
respected him. "The baby doesn't have to be in Daniel
Parish's life. We won't bother you ever again, I swear to
God. We just need a little money to get started. To move
on. He said he would help, and now I can't find him
anywhere." This made sense to me. Daniel was always travelling a lot – visiting writer at a school in Switzerland, trips
to Los Angeles that never resulted in anything.

'"Okay," I said. "I'll try to get in touch with him and see
what I can do. If he acknowledges that your story is
true . . ." But I already knew that it was, Lambiase! "If he
acknowledges that your story is true, maybe we can do

something." The girl wanted to know how she could best contact me. I told her I'd be in touch.

'I talked to Daniel that night on the phone. It was a good talk, and I didn't bring up Marian Wallace. He was solicitous of me, started making plans for our own baby's arrival. "Ismay," he said, "once the baby's here, I'm going to be a changed man." I had heard that before. "No, I'm serious," he insisted, "I'm definitely going to travel less. I'm going to stay at home, write more, take care of you and the potato." He was always a good talker and I wanted to believe that this was the night everything was going to change in my marriage. I decided right then and there that I would take care of the problem with Marian Wallace. I would find a way to buy her off.

'People in this town have always thought my family had more money than we actually did. Nic and I did have small trust funds, but it wasn't a ton. She used hers to buy the store, and I used mine to buy this house. What was left over from my side, my husband spent quickly. His first book sold well, but the ones after less so, and he always had champagne tastes and an inconsistent income. I'm only a schoolteacher. Daniel and I always looked rich, but we were poor.

'Down the hill, my sister had been dead for over a year and a half, and her husband was steadily drinking himself to death. Out of obligation to her, I would check on A.J. some nights. I'd let myself in, wipe the vomit off his face, and drag him to bed. One night, I go in. A.J. is passed out as usual. And *Tamerlane* is sitting on the table. I should say here that I was with him the day he found *Tamerlane*. Not that he ever offered to split the money with me, which probably would have been the decent thing to do. Cheap bastard never would have been at that estate sale if not for me. So I put A.J. to bed, and I go out to the living room to clean up the mess, and I wipe everything down, and the last thing I do, without even really thinking about it, is I slip the book into my bag.

'The next day, everyone is looking for *Tamerlane*, but I'm out of town. I've gone into Cambridge for the day. I go to Marian Wallace's dorm room, and I throw the book on her bed. I tell her, "Look, you can sell this. It's worth a lot of money." And she looks at the book dubiously, and she says, "Is it hot?" And I say, "No, it belongs to Daniel, and he wants you to have it, but you can never say where it came from. Bring it to an auction house or a rare-books dealer. Claim you found it in a used-books bin somewhere." I don't hear from Marian Wallace again for a while, and I think maybe that's the end of it.' Ismay's voice trails off.

'But it isn't?' Lambiase asks.

'No. She shows up at the house with Maya and the book just before Christmas. She says she's gone to every auction house and dealer in the Boston area, and none of them want to deal with the book because it doesn't have a provenance, and the cops have been calling about a stolen copy of *Tamerlane*. She takes the book from her bag and hands it to me. I throw it back at her. "What am I going to do with this?" Marian Wallace just shakes her head. The book lands on the floor, and the little girl picks it up and starts flipping through it, but no one's paying any attention to her. Marian Wallace's huge amber eyes fill with tears, and she

says, "Have you read *Tamerlane*, Mrs Parish? It's so sad." I
shake my head. "It's a poem about this Turkish conqueror
who trades the love of his life, this poor peasant girl, for
power." I roll my eyes at her, and I say, "Is that what you
think is happening here? Do you fancy yourself some poor
peasant girl, and I'm the mean wife who is keeping you
from the love of your life?"

"'No," she says. At this point, the baby is crying. Marian
says that the worst of it is that she knew what she was
doing. Daniel had come to her college for a reading. She
had loved that book, and when she slept with him she had
read his author biography a million times and she knew
perfectly well that he was married. "I've made so many
mistakes," she says. "I can't help you," I say. She shakes her
head and picks up the baby. "We'll be out of your way
now," she says. "Merry Christmas."

'And they leave. I'm pretty shaken up, so I go into the
kitchen to make myself some tea. When I get back out to
the living room, I notice that the little girl has left her backpack and *Tamerlane* is on the floor next to it. I pick up the
book. I'm thinking I'll just slip into A.J.'s apartment tomorrow or the next night and return it. That's when I notice it
is covered in crayon drawings. The little girl has ruined it! I
zip it into the bag and put it in my closet. I don't take pains
to hide it very much. I think maybe Daniel will find it and
ask me about it, but he never does. He never cares. That
night, A.J. calls me about the proper things to feed a baby.
He's got Maya at his apartment, and I agree to go over.'

'The day after that, Marian Wallace washes up by the
lighthouse,' Lambiase says.

'Yes, I wait to see if Daniel will say anything, to see if he will recognize the girl and claim the baby, but he doesn't. And I, coward that I am, never bring it up.'

Lambiase takes her in his arms. 'None of this matters,' he says after a while. 'If there was a crime—'

'There *was* a crime,' she insists.

'If there was a crime,' he repeats, 'everyone who knows about any of it is dead.'

'Except Maya.'

'Maya's life has turned out beautifully,' Lambiase says.

Ismay shakes her head. 'It has, hasn't it?'

'The way I see it,' Lambiase says, 'you saved A.J. Fikry's life when you stole that manuscript. That's the way I see it.'

'What kind of cop are you?' Ismay asks.

'The old kind,' he says.

The next night, like every third Wednesday of every month for the last ten years, is Chief's Choice at Island Books. At first, the police officers felt obligated to join, but the group has grown in genuine popularity over the years. Now it's the largest book meet-up that Island has. Police officers still make up the bulk of the membership, but their wives and even some of their children, when they get old enough, attend. Years ago, Lambiase had had to institute a 'leave your weapons' policy after a young cop had pulled a gun on another cop during a particularly heated discussion of *The House of Sand and Fog*. (Lambiase would later reflect to A.J. that the selection had been a mistake. 'Had an interesting cop character but too much moral ambiguity in that one. I'm going to stick to easier genre stuff from now on.') Other than this incident, the group has been free of violence. Aside from the content of the books, of course.

As is his tradition, Lambiase arrives at the store early to set up for Chief's Choice and talk to A.J. 'I saw this resting on the door,' Lambiase says when he comes inside. He hands a padded Manila envelope with A.J.'s name on it to his friend.

'Probably another galley,' A.J. says.

'Don't say that,' Lambiase jokes. 'Could be the next big thing in there.'

'Yeah, I'm sure. It's probably the Great American Novel. I'll add it to my stack: Things to Read before My Brain Stops Working.'

A.J. sets the package on the countertop, and Lambiase watches it. 'You never know,' Lambiase says.

'I'm like a girl who has been on the dating scene too long. I've had too many disappointments, too many promises of "the one", and they never are. As a cop, don't you get that way?'

'What way?'

'Cynical, I guess,' A.J. says. 'Don't you ever get to the point where you expect the worst from people all the time?'

Lambiase shakes his head. 'No. I see good people just as much as I see bad ones.'

'Yeah, name me some.'

'People like you, my friend.' Lambiase clears his throat, and A.J. can think of no reply. 'What's good in crime that I haven't read? I need some new picks for Chief's Choice.'

A.J. walks over to the Crime section. He looks across the spines, which are, for the most part, black and red with all capitalized fonts in silvers and whites. An occasional burst of fluorescence breaks up the monotony. A.J. thinks how similar everything in the crime genre looks. Why is any one book different from any other book? They are different, A.J. decides, because they are. We have to look inside many. We have to believe. We agree to be disappointed sometimes so that we can be exhilarated every now and again.

He selects one and holds it out to his friend. 'Maybe this?'

What We Talk about
When We Talk about Love

1980/Raymond Carver

Two couples get increasingly drunk; discuss what is and what is not love.

A question I've thought about a great deal is why it is so much easier to write about the things we dislike/hate/acknowledge to be flawed than the things we love.* This is my favourite short story, Maya, and yet I cannot begin to tell you why.

(You and Amelia are my favourite people, too.)

— A.J.F.

---

* This accounts for much of the Internet, of course.

'Lot 2200. A last-minute addition to the afternoon's auction and a rare opportunity for the vintage books connoisseur. *Tamerlane and Other Poems* by Edgar Allan Poe. Written when Poe was eighteen and attributed to "A Bostonian". Only fifty printed at the time. *Tamerlane* will be the crown jewel in any serious rare-books collection. This copy shows some wear at the spine and is marked in crayon on the cover. The damage should not in any way spoil the beauty or diminish the rarity of this object, which cannot be overstated. Let the bidding begin at twenty thousand dollars.'

The book sells for seventy-two thousand dollars, modestly exceeding the reserve. After fees and taxes, this is enough money to cover A.J.'s co-pay on the surgery and the first round of radiation.

Even after he receives the cheque from Christie's, A.J. has doubts about whether to go through with treatment. He still suspects that the money would be better spent on Maya's college education. 'No,' Maya says. 'I'm smart. I'll get a scholarship. I'll write the world's saddest admissions essay about how I was an orphan abandoned in a bookstore by my single mother and how my adopted dad got the rarest form of brain cancer, but look at me now. An upstanding member of society. People will eat it up, Dad.'

'That is awfully crass of you, my little nerd.' A.J. laughs at the monster he has created.

'I have money, too,' the wife insists. Bottom line is, the women in A.J.'s life want him to live, and so he books the surgery.

'Sitting here, I find myself thinking that *The Late Bloomer* really was a bunch of hokum,' Amelia says bitterly. She stands up and walks over to the window. 'Do you want the blinds raised or lowered? Raised, we get a spot of natural light and the lovely view of the children's hospital across the way. Lowered, you can enjoy my deathly pallor under the fluorescent lights. It's up to you.'

'Raised,' A.J. says. 'I want to remember you at your best.'

'Do you remember when Friedman writes how you can't truly describe a hospital room? How a hospital room when the one you love is in it is too painful to be described or some such crap? How did we ever think that was poetic? I'm disgusted with us. At this stage in my life, I'm with all the people that never wanted to read that book in the first place. I'm with the cover designer who put the flowers and the feet on the front. Because you know what? You totally can describe a hospital room. It's grey. The art is the worst art you've ever seen. Like stuff that got rejected by the Holiday Inn. Everything smells like someone is trying to cover up the smell of piss.'

'You loved *The Late Bloomer*, Amy.'

She has still never told him about Leon Friedman. 'But I didn't want to be in some stupid play version of it when I was in my forties.'

'Do you think I should really have this surgery?'

Amelia rolls her eyes. 'Yes, I do. Number one, it's happening in twenty minutes, so we probably couldn't get our money back anyway. And number two, you've had your head shaved, and you look like a terrorist. I don't see what the point is in turning back now,' Amelia says.

'Is it really worth the money for two more years that are likely to be crappy?' he asks Amelia.

'It is,' she says, taking his hand.

'I remember a woman who told me about the importance of shared sensibility. I remember a woman who said she broke up with a bona fide American Hero because they didn't have good conversation. That could happen to us, you know,' A.J. says.

'That is an entirely different situation,' Amelia insists. A second later, she yells, 'FUCK!' A.J. thinks something must be seriously wrong because Amelia never curses.

'What is it?'

'Well, the thing is, I rather like your brain.'

He laughs at her, and she weeps a little.

'Oh, enough with the tears. I don't want your pity.'

'I'm not crying for you. I'm crying for me. Do you know how long it took me to find you? Do you know how many awful dates I've been on? I can't' – she is breathless now – 'I can't join Match.com again. I just can't.'

'Big Bird – always looking ahead.'

'Big Bird. What the . . . ? You can't introduce a nickname at this point in our relationship!'

'You'll meet someone. I did.'

'Fuck you. I like you. I'm used to you. You are the one, you asshole. I can't meet someone new.'

He kisses her and then she reaches under his hospital gown between his legs and squeezes. 'I love having sex with you,' she says. 'If you're a vegetable when this is done, can I still have sex with you?' she asks.

'Sure,' A.J. says.

'And you won't think less of me?'

'No.' He pauses. 'I'm not sure I'm comfortable with the turn this conversation has taken,' he says.

'You knew me four years before you asked me out.'

'True.'

'You were so mean to me the day we met.'

'Also true.'

'I'm so screwed up. How will I ever find someone else?'

'You seem remarkably unconcerned about my brain.'

'Your brain's toast. We both know that. But what about me?'

'Poor Amy.'

'Yes, before I was a bookseller's wife. That was pitiable enough. Soon I'll be the bookseller's widow.'

She kisses him on every place of his malfunctioning head. 'I liked this brain. I like this brain! It is a very good brain.'

'Me too,' he says.

The attendant comes to wheel him away. 'I love you,' she says with a resigned shrug. 'I want to leave you with something cleverer than that, but it's all I know.'

When he wakes, he finds the words are more or less there. It takes a while to find some of them, but they are there.

Blood.

Painkiller.

Vomit.

Bucket.

Haemorrhoids.

Diarrhoea.

Water.

Blisters.

Diaper.

Ice.

After surgery, he is brought to an isolated wing of the hospital for a month-long course of radiation. His immune system is so compromised from the radiation that he isn't allowed any visitors. It is the loneliest he has ever been and that includes the period after Nic's death. He wishes he could get drunk, but his irradiated stomach couldn't take it. This is what life had been like before Maya and before Amelia. A man is not his own island. Or at least a man is not optimally his own island.

When he isn't throwing up or restlessly half sleeping, he digs out the e-reader his mother gave him last Christmas. (The nurses deem the e-reader to be more sanitary than a paper book. 'They should put that on the box,' A.J. quips.) He finds that he can't stay awake to read an entire novel. Short stories are better. He has always preferred short stories anyway. As he is reading, he finds that he wants to make a new list of short stories for Maya. She is going to be a writer, he knows. He is not a writer, but he has thoughts about the profession, and he wants to he tell her those things. *Maya, novels certainly have their charms, but the most elegant creation in the prose universe is a short story. Master the short story and you'll have mastered the world,* he thinks just before he drifts off to sleep. *I should write this down,* he thinks. He reaches for a pen, but there isn't one anywhere near the toilet bowl he is resting against.

At the end of the radiation treatment, the oncologist finds that his tumour has neither shrunk nor grown. He gives A.J. a year. 'Your speech and everything else will likely deteriorate,' he says in a voice that strikes A.J. as incongruously chipper. No matter, A.J. is glad to be going home.

The Bookseller

1986/Roald Dahl

Bonbon about a bookseller with an unusual way of extorting money from customers. In terms of characters, it is Dahl's usual collection of opportunistic grotesques. In terms of plot, the twist is a late-comer and not enough to redeem the story's flaws. 'The Bookseller' really shouldn't be on this list – it is not an exceptional Dahl offering in any way. Certainly no 'Lamb to the Slaughter' – and yet here it is. How to account for its presence when I know it is only average? The answer is this: Your dad relates to the characters. It has meaning to me. And the longer I do this (bookselling, yes, of course, but also living if that isn't too awfully sentimental), the more I believe that this is what the point of it all is. To connect, my dear little nerd. Only connect.

– A.J.F.

It is so simple, he thinks. *Maya*, he wants to say, *I have figured it all out.*

But his brain won't let him.

The words you can't find, you borrow.

We read to know we're not alone. We read because we are alone. We read and we are not alone. We are not alone.

My life is in these books, he wants to tell her. *Read these and know my heart.*

We are not quite novels.

The analogy he is looking for is almost there.

We are not quite short stories. At this point, his life is seeming closest to that.

In the end, we are collected works.

He has read enough to know there are no collections where each story is perfect. Some hits. Some misses. If you're lucky, a stand-out. And in the end, people only really remember the stand-outs anyway, and they don't remember those for very long.

No, not very long.

'Dad,' Maya says.

He tries to figure out what she is saying. The lips and the sounds. What can they mean?

Thankfully, she repeats, 'Dad.'

Yes, Dad. Dad is what I am. Dad is what I became. The father of Maya. Maya's dad. Dad. What a word. What a little big word.

What a word and what a world! He is crying. His heart is too full, and no words to release it. *I know what words do,* he thinks. *They let us feel less.*

'No, Dad. Please don't. It's okay.'

She puts her arms around him.

Reading has become difficult. If he tries very hard, he can still make it through a short story. Novels have become impossible. He can write more easily than he can speak. Not that writing is easy. He writes a paragraph a day. A paragraph for Maya. It isn't much, but it's what he has left to give.

He wants to tell her something very important.

'Does it hurt?' she asks.

No, he thinks. The brain has no pain sensors and so it can't hurt. The loss of his mind has turned out to be a curiously pain-free process. He feels that it ought to hurt more.

'Are you afraid?' she asks.

Not of dying, he thinks, *but a little of this part I'm in. Every day, there is less of me. Today I am thoughts without words. Tomorrow I will be a body without thoughts. And so it goes. But Maya, you are here right now and so I am glad to be here. Even without books and words. Even without my mind. How the hell do you say this? How do you even begin?*

Maya is staring at him and now she is crying, too.

'Maya,' he says. 'There is only one word that matters.' He looks at her to see if he has been understood. Her brow is furrowed. He can tell that he hasn't made himself clear. *Fuck.* Most of what he says is gibberish these days. If he wants to be understood, it is best to limit himself to one-word replies. But some things take longer than one word to explain.

He will try again. He will never stop trying. 'Maya, we are what we love. We are that we love.'

Maya is shaking her head. 'Dad, I'm sorry. I don't understand.'

'We aren't the things we collect, acquire, read. We are, for as long as we are here, only love. The things we loved. The people we loved. And these, I think these really do live on.'

She is still shaking her head. 'I can't understand you, Dad. I wish I could. Do you want me to get Amy? Or maybe you could try to type it?'

He is sweating. Conversing isn't fun any more. It used to be so easy. *All right,* he thinks. *If it's gotta be one word, it's gotta be one word.*

'Love?' he asks. He prays it has come out right.

She furrows her brow and tries to read his face. 'Gloves?' she asks. 'Are your hands cold, Dad?'

He nods, and she takes his hands in hers. His hands had been cold, and now they are warm, and he decides that he's gotten close enough for today. Tomorrow, maybe, he will find the words.

At the bookseller's funeral, the question on everyone's mind is what will become of Island Books. People are attached to their bookstores, more attached than A.J. Fikry ever would have guessed. It matters who placed *A Wrinkle in Time* in your twelve-year-old daughter's nail-bitten fingers or who sold you that *Let's Go* travel guide to Hawaii or who insisted that your aunt with the very particular tastes would surely adore *Cloud Atlas*. Furthermore, they like Island Books. And even though they aren't always perfectly faithful, even though they buy e-books sometimes and shop online, they like what it says about their town that Island Books is right in the centre of the main strip, that it's the second or third place you come to after you get off the ferry.

At the funeral, they approach Maya and Amelia, respectfully, of course, and whisper, 'A.J. can't ever be replaced but will you find someone else to run the store?'

Amelia doesn't know what to do. She loves Alice. She loves Island Books. She has no experience running a bookstore. She has always worked on the publisher side of things and she needs her steady pay cheque and health insurance even more now that she is responsible for Maya. She considers leaving the store open and letting someone else run it during the week, but the plan isn't tenable. The commute is too great, and what it really makes sense to do is move off the island altogether. After a week of heartsickness and bad sleep and intellectual pacing, she makes the decision to close the store. The store – the building the store is housed in and the land it sits on, at least – is worth a lot of money. (Nic and A.J. had bought it outright all those years ago.) Amelia loves Island Books, but she can't make it work. For a month or so, she makes attempts at selling the store, but no buyers come forward. She puts the building on the market. Island Books will close at the end of the summer.

'End of an era,' Lambiase says to Ismay over eggs at the local diner. He's broken-hearted over the news, but he's planning to leave Alice soon anyway. He will have done twenty-five years in the police force next spring, and he's got a fair amount of money saved up. He imagines himself buying a boat and living in the Florida Keys, like a retired cop character in an Elmore Leonard novel. He's been trying to convince Ismay to come with him, and he thinks he's starting to wear her down. Lately she's been finding fewer and fewer reasons to object, although she is one of those odd New England creatures who like the winter.

'I hoped they'd find someone else to run the store. But the truth is, Island Books wouldn't be the same without A.J., Maya and Amelia anyway,' Lambiase says. 'Wouldn't have the same heart.'

'True,' Ismay says. 'It's gross, though. They'll probably turn it into a Forever 21.'

'What's a Forever 21?'

Ismay laughs at him. 'How do you not know this? Wasn't it ever referenced in one of those YA novels you're always reading?'

'Young-adult fiction isn't like that.'

'It's a chain clothing store. Actually, we should be so lucky. They'll probably turn it into a bank.' She sips at her coffee. 'Or a drugstore.'

'Maybe a Jamba Juice?' Lambiase says. 'I love Jamba Juice.'

Ismay starts to cry.

The waitress stops by the table, and Lambiase indicates that she should clear the plates. 'I know how you feel,' Lambiase says. 'I don't like it either, Izzie. You know something funny about me? I never read much before I met A.J. and started going to Island. As a kid, the teachers thought I was a slow reader, so I never got the knack for it.'

'You tell a kid he doesn't like to read, and he'll believe you,' Ismay says.

'Mainly got Cs in English, too. Once A.J. adopted Maya, I wanted to have an excuse to go into the store to check on them, so I kept reading whatever he'd give me. And then I started to like it.'

Ismay cries harder.

'Turns out I really like bookstores. You know, I meet a lot of people in my line of work. A lot of folks pass through Alice Island, especially in the summer. I've seen movie people on vacation and I've seen music people and news people, too. There ain't nobody in the world like book people. It's a business of gentlemen and gentlewomen.'

'I wouldn't go that far,' Ismay says.

'I don't know, Izzie. I'm telling you. Bookstores attract the right kind of folk. Good people like A.J. and Amelia. And I like talking about books with people who like talking about books. I like paper. I like how it feels, and I like the feel of a book in my back pocket. I like how a new book smells, too.'

Ismay kisses him. 'You're the funniest sort of cop I ever met.'

'I worry about what Alice is going to be like if there isn't a bookstore here,' Lambiase says as he finishes his coffee.

'Me too.'

Lambiase leans across the table and kisses her on the cheek. 'Hey, here's a crazy thought. What if, instead of going to Florida, you and me took over the place?'

'In this economy, that *is* a crazy thought,' Ismay says.

'Yeah,' he says. 'Probably so.' The waitress asks if they want dessert. Ismay says she doesn't want anything, but

Lambiase knows she'll always share a little of his. He orders a slice of cherry pie, two forks.

'But, you know, what if we did?' Lambiase continues. 'I've got savings and a pretty good pension about to come in, and so do you. And A.J. said the summer people always bought a lot of books.'

'The summer people have e-readers now,' Ismay counters.

'True,' Lambiase says. He decides to let the subject drop.

They are halfway through their pie when Ismay says, 'We could open a cafe, too. That would probably help with the bottom line.'

'Yeah, A.J. used to talk about that sometimes.'

'And,' Ismay says, 'we turn the basement into a theatre space. That way, the author events don't have to be right in the middle of the store. Maybe people could even rent it as a theatre or meeting space sometimes, too.'

'Your theatre background would be great for that,' Lambiase says.

'Are you sure you're up to this? We aren't super-young,' Ismay says. 'What about no winters? What about Florida?'

'We'll go there when we're old. We're not old yet,' Lambiase says after a pause. 'I've lived in Alice my whole life. It's the only place I've ever known. It's a nice place, and I intend to keep it that way. A place ain't a place without a bookstore, Izzie.'

Not long after she sells the store to Ismay and Lambiase, Amelia decides to leave Knightley Press. Maya is graduating from high school, and Amelia is tired of travelling so much.

She finds a position as a book buyer for a large general retailer out of Maine. Before she leaves, as her predecessor Harvey Rhodes had done, Amelia writes up notes on all her active accounts. She saves Island Books for last.

'Island Books,' she reports. 'Owners: Ismay Parish (ex-school teacher) and Nicholas Lambiase (ex-police chief). Lambiase is an exceptional hand seller, especially of literary crime fiction and young-adult novels. Parish, who used to run the high school drama club, can be counted on to throw an A+ author event. The store has a cafe, a stage, and an excellent online presence. All this was built on the solid foundation established by A.J. Fikry, the original owner, whose tastes ran more toward the literary. The store still carries a ton of literary fiction, but the owners won't take what they can't sell. I love Island Books with all my heart. I do not believe in God. I have no religion. But this to me is as close to a church as I have known in this life. It is a holy place. With bookstores like this, I feel confident in saying that there will be a book business for a very long time. – Amelia Loman'

Amelia feels a bit embarrassed about those last several sentences and cuts everything after 'the owners won't take what they can't sell'.

'... the owners won't take what they can't sell.' Jacob Gardner reads his predecessor's notes one last time, then clicks off his phone and disembarks from the ferry with long, purposeful strides. Jacob, twenty-seven years old and armed with a half-paid-off master's degree in non-fiction writing, is ready. He can't believe his luck in landing this job.

Sure, the pay could be better, but he loves books, has always loved books. He believes that they saved his life. He even has that famous C. S. Lewis quote tattooed on his wrist. Imagine getting to be one of those people who actually get paid to talk about literature. He'd do this for free, not that he wants his publisher to know that. He needs the money. Living in Boston isn't cheap, and he's only doing this day job to support his passion: his oral history of gay vaudevillians. But this isn't to take away from the fact that Jacob Gardner is nothing short of a believer. He even walks like he has a calling. He could be mistaken for a missionary. In point of fact, he was raised Mormon, but this is another story.

Island is Jacob's first sales call, and he can't wait to get there. He can't wait to tell them about all the great books he's carrying in his Knightley Press tote bag. The bag must weigh almost fifty pounds, but Jacob works out and he isn't even feeling it. Knightley's got a remarkably strong list this year, and he's certain his job will be easy. Readers are going to have no choice but to love these titles. The nice woman who hired him had suggested he start with Island Books. The owner there loves literary crime fiction, eh? Well, Jacob's favourite from the list is a debut about an Amish girl who disappears while on Rumspringa, and in Jacob's opinion, it's a must-read for all serious lovers of literary crime fiction.

As Jacob passes over the threshold of the purple Victorian cottage, the wind chimes play their familiar song and a gruff, but not unfriendly, voice calls, 'Welcome.'

Jacob walks down the history aisle and holds out his hand to the middle-aged man on the ladder. 'Mr Lambiase, have I got a book for you!'

To buy any of our books and to find out
more about Abacus and Little, Brown, our authors
and titles, as well as events and book clubs,
visit our website

www.littlebrown.co.uk

and follow us on Twitter

@AbacusBooks
@LittleBrownUK

To order any Abacus titles p & p free in the UK,
please contact our mail order supplier on:

+ 44 (0)1832 737525

Customers not based in the UK should contact
the same number for appropriate postage
and packing costs.